I... **ruel mouth. A mouth she wanted on hers.**

His eyes snapped open, then went unerringly to her face. The heat she saw there was unmistakable. It nearly fixed her feet to the spot, but she forced herself to move as if nothing was any different. As if they were still Miss Black and Mr. D'Angeli, and this was simply a morning at the office and she was taking him coffee.

Faith set her own drink down and turned back to him. The look in his eyes scorched her, made her long for things she knew she could not have. Things she should not want. She'd been nearly ruined once in her desire to please a man. She would never forget herself again. What she wanted was more important than what a man might want from her.

Men could not be trusted.

Renzo reached up and took her hand in his. Her skin sizzled as fire snaked through her.

"You feel it too," he said. "I know you do."

"Renzo—" she began, but he bent and fitted his gorgeous mouth to hers, silencing her.

Lynn Raye Harris read her first Mills & Boon®
romance when her grandmother carted home a box
from a yard sale. She didn't know she wanted to be
a writer then, but she definitely knew she wanted to
marry a sheikh or a prince and live the glamorous
life she read about in the pages. Instead she married
a military man, and moved around the world. These
days she makes her home in North Alabama, with her
handsome husband and two crazy cats. Writing for
Harlequin Mills & Boon is a dream come true. You can
visit her at www.lynnrayeharris.com

Books by Lynn Raye Harris:

MARRIAGE BEHIND THE FAÇADE
CAPTIVE BUT FORBIDDEN
STRANGERS IN THE DESERT

Did you know these are also available as eBooks?
Visit www.millsandboon.co.uk

UNNOTICED
AND UNTOUCHED

BY
LYNN RAYE HARRIS

MILLS
BOON

First published in Great Britain 2011
by Mills & Boon, an imprint of Harlequin (UK) Limited.
Harlequin (UK) Limited, Eton House, 18-24 Paradise Road,
Richmond, Surrey TW9 1SR

© Lynn Raye Harris 2012

ISBN: 978 0 263 89089 1

Harlequin (UK) policy is to use papers that are natural, renewable
and recyclable products and made from wood grown in sustainable for-
ests. The logging and manufacturing process conform to the
legal environmental regulations of the country of origin.

Printed and bound in Spain
by Blackprint CPI, Barcelona

UNNOTICED
AND UNTOUCHED

To the men in my life—my husband, Mike, who has never met a sport he didn't like (and who patiently attempts to explain the rules to me every time), and to my dad and father-in-law, who both love motor sports. I still don't get that hockey thing, and I'll never understand what makes baseball on television so fascinating, or why anyone wants to watch cars go in circles for hours. But I do, finally, mostly understand American football. I think.

CHAPTER ONE

"Miss Black, you will accompany me this evening."

Faith's head snapped up. Her boss, Lorenzo D'Angeli, stood in the doorway to his office, looking every bit the arrogant Italian businessman in his custom suit and handmade loafers. Her heart skipped a beat as she contemplated his gorgeous face—all hard angles and sharp planes, deeply bronzed skin, and eyes as sharp and clear blue as a Georgia spring sky. It wasn't the first time—and likely wouldn't be the last—but it irritated her that she reacted that way.

She knew all about men like him. Arrogant, entitled and selfish—she had only to look at the way he treated the women who paraded in and out of his life with ruthless regularity to know it was the truth, in spite of the fact he'd only ever been courteous to her.

"The dress is formal," he continued. "If you need clothing, take the afternoon off and charge your purchases to my account."

Faith's heart was skipping in earnest now. She'd often gone shopping for her boss in the six months she'd worked for him, purchasing silk ties or gold cuff links at his direction or picking up little gifts for whatever woman he was seeing at the time, but he'd never told her to shop for herself. It was, without question, unusual.

And perfectly impossible.

"I'm sorry, Mr. D'Angeli," she said as politely as she could, "but I don't believe I understand you."

His stance didn't soften an inch. "Miss Palmer is no longer going. I need a date."

Faith stiffened. Of course. But stepping in because he'd had a fight with yet another woman he was sleeping with was not part of her job description.

"Mr. D'Angeli," she began.

"Faith, I need you."

Four words. Four words that somehow managed to stop the breath in her chest and send a tremor over her. Oh, why did she let him get to her? Why did the mere thought of parading around town on his arm make her feel weak when he was the last person she would ever want to be with?

She forced herself to think logically. He wasn't saying he needed *her*. He needed the efficient PA at his side, ever ready to make calls or take notes or rearrange his schedule at a moment's notice.

He did not need the woman. Lorenzo D'Angeli needed no woman, she reminded herself.

"It's highly inappropriate, Mr. D'Angeli. I cannot go."

"Faith, you are the only woman I can count on," he said. "The only one who does not play games with me."

Her ears burned. For God's sake. Narcissus himself hadn't been that self-focused. "I don't play games because I'm your personal assistant, Mr. D'Angeli."

"Precisely why I need you with me tonight. I can trust you to behave."

Behave? She wanted to smack him. Instead, she gave him an even look, though her pulse was racing along like one of the superbikes that had made D'Angeli Motors famous. For as long as she lived, she'd never understand how she let this man get to her. He was darn pretty to look at, but he believed everything revolved around him.

Including her, it would seem.

"Shall I ring Miss Zachetti for you? Or Miss Price? I'm sure they're available. And if they are not, they certainly will be when they realize who's calling."

They'd fall all over themselves for another night in his company, Faith thought, frowning. She hadn't yet met a woman who wouldn't.

Renzo stalked toward her desk. Then he put his palms on it and leaned down until his eyes were nearly on a level with hers. She could smell his cologne, that expensive scent of man and spice and sleek machine that she always associated with him. No matter how beautifully groomed he was, how perfect, he still had an edge of wildness that made her think of the motorcycles he both built and raced.

He was famous the world over for his cool. Famous for staring down death at two hundred plus miles an hour on the track with nothing between him and the asphalt but a bit of leather, steel and carbon fiber. This was the man who'd won five world titles before a severe crash left him with pins in his leg and a cane that doctors said he would always need to walk.

But of course he hadn't accepted that fate. He'd worked hard to lose the cane, and even harder to get back on the racetrack. His determination had netted him four more world titles and the nickname of the Iron Prince. Iron because he was unbreakable and Prince because he ruled the track.

And now that iron-willed, determined, unbreakable man was staring at her with eyes so blue and piercing that she dropped her gaze nervously in spite of her determination not to. Faith reached for the telephone, her heart pounding in her throat.

"Which lucky lady will it be?" she asked, cursing herself for the falsetto note that betrayed her agitation.

Renzo's hand lashed out, lay against hers where it rested on the receiver. His skin was warm—shockingly so, she thought, as her flesh seemed to sizzle and burn beneath his. A surge of energy passed through her fingers, her wrist, up her forearm, down her torso and up her spine at the same time. Her body responded with a tightening that was very much unlike her.

"There is a bonus in it for you, Miss Black," Renzo said, his voice silky smooth as it caressed her name. "Whatever clothing you buy, you may keep. And I shall pay you one month's salary for complying with my simple request. This is good, *si?*"

Faith closed her eyes. Good? It was great. A month's extra pay would look very good in her bank account. It would put her that much closer to being able to buy a condo for herself instead of renting an apartment. When she had her own place, she'd finally feel like she'd accomplished something. Like she'd left the Georgia clay behind and made something of herself, in spite of her father's pronouncement that she never would amount to anything.

But she should still refuse. Wherever Lorenzo D'Angeli went, there were photographers and media and attention. She didn't want or need that, hadn't ever worried about it as a PA in an office. But as the woman on his arm, no matter that it was simply a job?

It wouldn't matter that it wasn't real. Her picture would be taken. She could end up on the front page of some tabloid....

And just as quickly the photo would disappear. It was one night, not a lifetime. What were the chances anyone would see a photo of Faith Black and connect her to Faith Louise Winston?

Poor, disgraced Faith Winston. She shivered inwardly. She would not live her life in fear of that single mistake returning to the fore. She was a grown woman now, not a naive teenager.

"Where is the event?" she asked, cursing herself even as she did so. It was a crack in her resolve, and he knew it.

The pressure of Renzo's hand eased, fell away. His eyes gleamed hotter than before—or perhaps she was hallucinating. Yes, of course. Hallucinating. Because there was no way he was looking at her with heat in his gaze.

"Manhattan," he said. "Fifth Avenue." He stood to his full height, and she tilted her head back to look up at him. A satisfied smile lifted the corners of his sensual mouth. "Please be ready by seven, Miss Black. My car will call for you then."

"I have not agreed to go," she said, her mouth as dry as a desert—but they both knew she was on the precipice of surrender. Yet some stubborn part of her refused to cave in so easily. Everything came so effortlessly to this man, and she had no desire to be yet another thing that fell into his lap simply because he wanted it to happen. The one time she'd allowed a man to talk her into something she'd been reluctant to do, the consequences had been disastrous.

But this man was her boss. He was not pretending an affection he did not feel simply to get her to comply with his request. And she was no longer an impressionable eighteen-year-old—how disastrous could the consequences really be?

"You have nothing to lose, Faith," Renzo said, his accent sliding over her name so sensuously that she shivered in spite of herself. "And much to gain."

"This is not part of my job description," she insisted, clinging to that one truth in the face of his beautiful persuasion.

"No, it is not."

They stared at each other without speaking—and then he bent to her level again, palms on the desk once more.

"You would be doing me a great favor," he said. "And you would be helping D'Angeli Motors in the process."

And then he smiled that killer smile of his, the one that made supermodels, nubile actresses and picture-perfect beauty queens swoon in delight. She was alarmed to realize she was not as unaffected as she'd always supposed she would be.

"You are of course free to refuse, but I would be most grateful to you, Faith, if you did not."

"This is not a date," she said firmly. "It's business."

He laughed, and she felt the heat of embarrassment slip through her. Why had she said that? Of course he wouldn't see her as a *real* date. She was too plain to ever be taken seriously as his date, but if he wanted to pay her to pretend, then fine. So long as they kept everything on a business foundation, she'd take the money and run.

"*Assolutamente, cara,*" Renzo said, gifting her once more with that smile, with the laser intensity of deep blue eyes boring into hers. "Now please, take the afternoon off. Go to Saks. My car will take you."

"I'm sure I can find something suitable in my closet," she insisted.

His look said he doubted it. "You happen to have the latest designer attire in your closet, Miss Black? Something appropriate for a gathering of New York's elite?"

Shame coiled within her. He paid her quite well, but she wasn't a fashionista. Not only that, but she had a condo to save for and no need to wear a formal gown. Until now. "Probably not," she admitted.

His smile was indulgent, patient. "Then go. This is part of the deal, Miss Black."

He disappeared behind his office door as if he had no doubts she would obey. Faith wanted to protest, but instead she sighed. And then she logged off her computer and gathered her purse. She'd launched herself into the deep end. She had no choice but to sink or swim.

Renzo's leg ached tonight. He set his laptop aside and rubbed his hand against the pain as the Escalade moved through Brooklyn traffic on the way to his PA's apartment. The discomfort was growing worse as the months went by, not better. He swore softly. His doctors had told him this might happen, but he'd worked too hard to let everything he'd gained slide away. He'd defeated the pain once; he would do so again.

He curled his hand into a fist and dug into the muscle. He wasn't finished yet. He refused to be.

Niccolo Gavretti of Gavretti Manufacturing was his biggest competitor, and Niccolo would love nothing more than to see Renzo lose not only the next world title but also D'Angeli's domination of the market. Renzo frowned as he thought of Niccolo. They'd been friends once, or at least Renzo had thought they had.

He knew better now.

And he would not lose. *He* would be the one to take the D'Angeli Viper onto the track and prove that he'd created the greatest superbike the racing world had ever seen—once the kinks in the design were worked out—and he would win another world title in the process.

His investors would be happy, the money would keep flowing and the next production version would be a huge hit with the public. Then Renzo would gladly retire from racing and leave it to the D'Angeli team to continue to dominate the motorcycle Grand Prix circuit.

Dio, per favore, one last title—one last victory—and he would stop.

Tonight was critical to his success, and he hoped he had not made a mistake in asking his plain but efficient secretary to accompany him. Desperate times, however, called for desperate measures.

He could appear at Robert Stein's party alone, of course. Perhaps everything would be fine if he did. But he had no desire to spend the evening avoiding Stein's daughter. Lissa was too young, too spoiled and too obvious in her attention.

And Robert Stein did not seem to appreciate his daughter's interest in Renzo one tiny bit. Though Renzo did not normally care what fathers thought, in this case he wanted it clear that he had no interest in Lissa Stein. For that, he'd needed a date, a woman who would stay close to his side and do his bidding when asked.

Everything had been perfect until this morning when he'd found himself saying the words to Katie Palmer that he usually said to a woman he'd grown tired of. He'd dated her for a month now, and she'd started to grow too clingy. The makeup bag tucked into one corner of his bathroom vanity wasn't too bad, nor was the toothbrush. Yet it was the shiny pink ladies' razor with several refills in his shower that, oddly enough, had been the last straw.

He had no problem with a woman spending the night when he invited her to do so. He was, however, quite irritated to find one starting to move herself in piece by piece after only a dozen nights together. Sex was an important and fulfilling aspect of his life, but he saw no need to confuse the issue with cohabitation. Renzo did not need to live with a woman to enjoy her, and he always made it clear in the beginning what his expectations were. Whenever someone crossed that line, they were summarily dismissed from his life.

Katie Palmer was a beautiful woman, an exciting woman, and yet she'd begun to leave him cold even before the pink razor and its endless refills had appeared. He wasn't quite sure why. She was exactly the sort of woman he usually dated—beautiful, slightly superficial and intellectually undemanding.

Renzo picked up his laptop again and stared at the report he'd been working on. He should have perhaps taken Faith's suggestion to invite a former girlfriend tonight instead of pressing her into service, but when the idea had first struck him as he'd sat at his desk and stared at a neatly typed memo with a helpful sticky note arrow pointing to the line for his signature, he'd had a sudden idea that taking his capable, mousy little PA with him would be far more productive than taking a woman who expected him to pay attention to her.

If he took Faith, it was business. She was a quiet, competent girl. She was not necessarily unattractive, he supposed, but he'd never really looked at her for signs of beauty. Why would he? She was his PA, and she was quite good at her job. His calendar had never been so orderly or his appointments so seamless.

Faith was perfect, even if she wasn't much to look at. She wore severe suits in dark colors that hid whatever figure she might have and scraped her golden hair back into ponytails and buns. She looked, truth be told, like a box. She also wore dark-rimmed spectacles.

But her eyes were green. He'd noticed that before, whenever she'd looked up at him through her glasses, her gaze sparking with intelligence. They were not dark like an emerald, but golden green like a spring leaf. And she smelled nice. Like an early-morning rain mingled with exotic flowers. There was no sharp perfume, no stale smell of smoke or alcohol or tanning solution.

But when she'd looked up at him this afternoon, her eyes flashing and a blush spreading over her cheeks, he'd had one wild, inconceivable moment when he'd imagined pulling her across the desk and fitting his mouth to hers.

Which made no sense. Faith Black was neat and efficient and smelled nice, but she wasn't the kind of woman he preferred. He liked her because she was professional and excellent at everything she did. He was not attracted to her.

It was, he supposed, an anomaly. A sign of the stress he'd been under for the past few months as his engineers worked to bring the Viper to top form. There were problems that had to be worked out or the bike would fail on the track.

And Renzo refused to accept failure. He'd poured a great deal of money and time into the development of this motorcycle, and he needed it to succeed. Success was everything. He'd known that since he was a teenager, since he'd realized that he actually *had* a father but that his father had not wanted to know him.

Because he wasn't a blue blood like the Conte de Lucano, or like the *conte*'s children with his wife. Renzo was the outcast, the unfortunate product of a somewhat hasty affair with a waitress. He hadn't been supposed to succeed—but he had, spectacularly, and he had every intention of continuing to do so.

Lorenzo D'Angeli never backed down from a challenge. He lived for them, thrived on them.

The limousine came to a halt in front of a plain concrete apartment building in a somewhat shabby neighborhood. Renzo winced as he moved his leg. It ached enough that he should allow his chauffeur to retrieve Faith, but he was just stubborn enough to refuse to permit even that small moment of vulnerability.

The car door opened and Renzo stepped onto the pavement, looking right and left, surveying the street and the people. The area didn't seem unsafe, yet it was worn. An unwanted memory tugged at his mind as he stood there. Another time, another place.

Another life, when he'd had nothing and had to struggle to feed his mother and younger sister. He'd been angry then, terribly angry. He'd always thought that if his mother had been more forceful, more demanding, she could have at least gotten the *conte* to make sure they had food and shelter. But she was weak, his mother, though he loved her completely. Too weak to fight back when she should have done so.

He ruthlessly squashed the feelings of helplessness the memory dredged up. Then he strode into the building and made his way to Faith's apartment on the second floor. There was no elevator. Renzo took the stairs quickly, in spite of the sharp throb in his leg. When he reached Faith's door, he took a moment to blank the pain from his mind before he rapped sharply.

She answered right away, the door whipping open to reveal a woman who might have made his jaw drop had he not had better control of himself. Faith Black was…different. A small spike of *something*—he did not know quite what—ricocheted through him as he studied her. She had not transformed into a voluptuous goddess, but she had transformed. Somehow.

The glasses were gone, and she was wearing makeup. He wasn't certain she ever wore makeup at the office, though perhaps she did. If she did, it wasn't quite like this, he was certain. Her lips were red, full and shiny from her lip gloss. Kissable.

Kissable?

"Mr. D'Angeli," she said, blinking in surprise.

"You were expecting someone else?" he asked mildly,

and yet the thought of her doing so caused a twinge of irritation to stab into him. Odd.

"I—well, yes. I had thought you were sending your car. I had thought I was meeting you at the event."

"As you see, this is not the case." He let his gaze drop slowly before meeting her pretty eyes again. She seemed surprised—and somewhat annoyed. She'd never been anything but professional in all their interactions, but what he saw in her eyes now made him wonder if it was possible that she did not like him.

Impossibile. Of course she did. He'd yet to meet a woman who didn't. He turned his best smile on her. "You look quite delightful, Miss Black."

And delectable, he was shocked to realize.

Her hair was piled on her head, but it wasn't quite as scraped back as usual; instead she'd pulled it into an elegant twist from which one disobedient tendril had escaped to lie against her cheek. Her pale lavender gown was demure, with a high neck, but it was also sleeveless and molded to her full breasts before falling away in ripples of fabric to the floor.

It was disconcerting, to say the least, to realize that she had a shape—and that shape was not a box. Quite the contrary, she was a study in curves, from the soft curve of her jaw to the curve of her bosom and down to the curve of her hips that he could just make out beneath the flowing fabric of her gown. He couldn't quite take his eyes from her, as if she might change back into the creature he knew if he looked away.

Color stained her cheeks as her green gaze fell from his. Satisfaction rippled through him. She was not immune after all. "Thank you. I—I was just searching for my earring backing. I dropped it and I'm not sure where it's gone."

He noticed then that she was only wearing one small

diamond earring. "Allow me to help," he said, pushing the door wider. She stepped back somewhat reluctantly, but she let him inside.

The apartment was small, but neat. The furnishings were worn, and there were a variety of magazines piled on a central table—including a couple of motorcycle magazines, it amused him to note. He was on the cover of the topmost one, in full leathers, looking grim as he stood beside a prototype of the Viper. And with good reason, considering the bike had fallen far short of what he'd been aiming for when he'd taken it out on the track. Not that the reporter had known, of course.

He dragged his gaze away from the magazine, continuing his study of Faith's home. A shelf stacked high with books ran along one short wall. The walls were industrial white, but she'd tried to punch it up with bright pictures and pillows on the furniture. It was a decidedly feminine space, though not in any overt way.

He thought of his mother decorating their tiny apartment in Positano with garlands of flowers and pretty fabric, and his jaw hardened as his thoughts turned dark. Did Faith also bring home an endless parade of men she hoped would fall in love with her? Did she cry at the end of the night—or series of nights—when she realized the current man was gone and never coming back?

"Over here," Faith said, leading the way to a tiny kitchen, which had barely enough room for two adults to stand together.

Her fragrance surrounded him as he joined her, that soft fresh scent he'd come to identify with her over the past few months. A sharp sensation rolled through him.

"I dropped it here," she said. "And it's rolled somewhere. It can't have gone far."

For a moment, he wasn't sure what they were talking

about. For a moment, for the barest of seconds, he wanted to press her soft body against the counter with his, wanted to drag the pins from her hair and see the golden mass tumble free. He shook the thought from his mind and focused on the task at hand.

"If you will allow me," he said, taking out his mobile phone and starting the application that turned the camera flash into a steady beam of light.

She couldn't leave the small space without brushing against him. A sliver of pleasure passed through him at the brief contact. *Stress*, he thought. *Simply stress.*

"And why were you putting on your earrings in the kitchen, Miss Black?" he asked as he stooped, ignoring the pain in his leg, and swept the light back and forth across the floor.

"I was in a hurry," she said. "I wanted to make it down to the street by the time your car arrived."

He tilted his head back to glance up at her. "You were planning to stand outside? Dressed like this?"

She shrugged. "I would have stood inside the building until I saw the car, but yes. I'm sorry you had to come up and get me."

The light flickered over something that glinted gold. Renzo swept the light into a corner again, found the small backing. He picked it up and pushed himself to his feet.

He gritted his teeth against the agony of spasming muscles and aching bone. "Miss Black, I am many things, not all of them pleasant, but I would hope that you realize I am not so callous as to make a lady wait in a dark and drafty hallway for my arrival."

"No, of course not," she said quietly, and he knew he must have looked severe. Yet he could not tell her why. Not without admitting what he would admit to no one—that he was weak, vulnerable, not made of iron after all.

Her gaze fell from his as she held her hand out to receive the tiny backing.

Renzo stared at the top of her golden head for a moment. He could have dropped it into her palm. That would have been easy. Prudent even. But he found he wanted to touch her again, wanted to see if he felt that same tiny jolt that he had this afternoon when he'd put his hand on hers before she could pick up the telephone. He'd dismissed the sensation as something akin to static electricity.

He put his fingers around her wrist and she gasped, her fingers curling inward on reflex before she forced them open again. He held her hand steady while he placed the backing in her palm. Her skin was soft, warm, and he wondered if the rest of her was equally as soft. Shockingly, a sliver of need began to tingle at the base of his spine. Renzo dropped her hand as if it had suddenly turned into a flaming brand.

Dio.

Her eyes were wide before she turned away. Her fingers shook as she fastened her earring in place, and he knew she must be affected, too. What was this sudden chemistry? Where had it come from? And why did he want to touch her again just so he could feel the jolt?

"There," she said unnecessarily when she completed the task. "I'm ready."

"Then we should be going," he said crisply. He helped her into her wrap and then waited while she locked the door. He had her precede him down the stairs, so that if he limped she would not know.

When they reached the street, his driver was standing at the ready with the door open. Renzo held his hand out to help Faith inside, but she did not take it, climbing into the custom Escalade on her own. He slid into the white leather seat beside her, and the door closed with a heavy thud.

They'd been gliding through the streets toward Manhattan for several minutes before she spoke. "Is there anything I should know about tonight, Mr. D'Angeli?"

Renzo glanced over at her. She was looking up at him with that focused look she usually got whenever he went over the morning reports with her.

Familiar ground, *grazie a Dio*. Perhaps now he could stop thinking about the way she smelled, about how delicate and feminine she seemed when he'd never quite noticed that about her before. Why had he noticed it now?

"We are attending a dinner at Robert Stein's residence," he said. "I am sure you realize why this is important."

She gave a firm nod. "Stein Engineering has patented a new form of racing tire. You wish them to build tires exclusively for the Viper instead of using stock tires. It would be an advantageous partnership."

"Ah, so you do pay attention in the meetings," he teased.

She looked surprised. And somewhat offended. "Of course I do. It's what you pay me for, Mr. D'Angeli."

Yes, it was what he paid her for. And tonight, he was paying her for something different. He, Lorenzo D'Angeli, was paying a woman to pretend to be his date. It was ludicrous, and yet he found he was rather looking forward to the evening in a way he would not have been had Katie Palmer been sitting beside him.

The Katie Palmers of the world were too obvious in their desire to own him, too certain of their sex appeal, and too jealous of his time and attention. He always found it amusing at first, but he quickly tired of it.

He knew it was his own fault, because that was the sort of woman he chose. But he'd watched his sweet, fragile mother pine for love for years, and he'd watched her be hurt again and again. She took things too seriously, thought every new man was her savior.

Because of that, Renzo had studiously avoided the kind of women in his own life who couldn't understand that sex was sex and love didn't enter the equation. He didn't believe in love, or at least not romantic love. If romantic love was real, then his mother should have found happiness years ago.

Faith wasn't like the women he usually dated. She wasn't superficial—and she wasn't fragile, either. In fact, she was looking at him now with what he thought might be thinly veiled disgust. A hot feeling blossomed inside him.

A challenge. He loved challenges.

Renzo couldn't quite stop himself from doing what he did next, if only to ruffle her cool. He reached for Faith's hand, took it in his while he traced small circles in her palm with his thumb. Her breath drew in sharply, and he could feel a tremor slide through her body. A current of satisfaction coiled within him. She was not impervious, no matter how hostile she looked, and that pleased him.

"Do you not think, *cara mia,*" he purred, "that you should perhaps call me Renzo?"

CHAPTER TWO

FAITH's skin sizzled beneath his touch, as if someone had dropped cool water onto hot coals. Her breath froze in her chest, and her voice refused to work as he traced little whorls in her palm. His hand was warm and solid, his thumb perhaps the most sensual thing she'd ever experienced as it moved softly against her skin.

Faith blinked as if it were a mirage that would disappear as soon as she did so. It did not.

Surely, then, she was asleep in her bed, dreaming that Renzo D'Angeli was holding her hand and speaking in a sultry voice that entreated her to call him by his first name.

Because this could not be real. She'd worked for him for six months, and he'd never once shown the slightest bit of interest in her as a woman. Not that she'd ever wanted him to. He was precisely the sort of man she despised the most: handsome, arrogant and certain he was entitled to excessive adoration.

But he was not noticing her in that way. It was impossible. He was simply playing along with the expectation they would be less formal together when she was posing as his date.

Yes, that must be it. Of course.

"I will try, Mr. D—Renzo," she said quietly, her heart beating in her ears.

"Much better," he said, smiling his lady-killer smile. But the thumb didn't stop moving and a tendril of heat made its way up her arm and down through her core, pooling in the deepest, most secretive part of her. It figured. Of all the men to affect her, it would be this one. A man she couldn't have in a bazillion years, even if she'd wanted him.

Which she did not. He was gorgeous, but about as trustworthy as the viper he'd named his motorcycle after.

She wanted him to let her go. And she didn't. The languidness stealing over her at his touch was addictive. What would she feel if he pulled her into his arms and kissed her? Would she lose her mind the way his other women did?

The thought was not a pleasant one. She'd already lost her mind over a man—or at least everyone thought she had—and she had no desire to experience that ever again. One second of stupidity, and Jason Moore had shattered her trust in men—in people—forever.

She was just about to ask Renzo to let her go when his phone rang.

"*Perdono*," he said before he took the call.

Faith folded her hands over her evening bag and watched the news ticker on the muted television screen across from her. That had been close. She didn't like feeling even remotely attracted to this man. She pictured Katie Palmer sashaying out of his office just a few days ago, lipstick smudged, hair mussed, and felt her dislike of him swell.

Yes. That was precisely how it was supposed to be.

Faith shifted in her seat. She'd ridden in his limo before, accompanying him to meetings across town, but this was the first time she'd sat here in an evening gown. When she'd gone to Saks today, she'd been surprised to be met by a personal shopper whom Renzo had arranged for her.

Faith had viewed gown after gown, the personal shopper growing perplexed, to say the least, when she refused the more daring dresses that showed too much cleavage or leg. Obviously Renzo had a preferred style he liked his women to wear. And Faith had been determined to wear what she liked, regardless of who was paying for the gown.

When the woman had brought the lavender gown out, Faith had known it was the one. When she put this dress on, she felt elegant, pretty and demure enough to please even her upright father.

Renzo finished his phone call and turned to her. "I need you to stay by my side tonight," he said. "It is very important that you do so."

Faith swallowed. "Of course, Mr—Renzo."

She could see his frown in the light from the television. "I'm counting on you, Faith. You have never failed me yet."

But she *had* disappointed him when she'd nearly called him Mr. D'Angeli again, and it bothered her. Because this was part of the job and he expected her to be able to do what he asked. It shouldn't be difficult, yet she was letting her nerves get the best of her.

Faith turned her head to look out the window as she pressed her fingernails into her palm and dug in. She would do a good job. Because he'd asked her to, and she'd agreed. She owed him that much. Tonight was important to the success of the Viper.

She knew that the Viper meant everything to him. How many times had she left the office late while he was still there, only to come in the next morning and find he'd never left? He worked hard on the designs, worked with his team to implement the changes that were required to make the motorcycle a success, and he worked hard on the business of running D'Angeli Motors.

D'Angeli wasn't only known for its racing bikes, of course. They also made production motorcycles that were popular with enthusiasts everywhere. Sales were growing steadily in the States, though perhaps not as quickly as Renzo would like. She knew she counted on the Viper to usher in a new wave of prosperity and growth for his company. And what was good for D'Angeli Motors was also good for her. For all his employees.

His phone rang again. He looked at the display and swore in Italian before sending the call to voice mail.

A woman, no doubt. Probably Katie Palmer. Katie was an underwear model, Faith recalled. If Renzo couldn't be satisfied with a woman who looked that good naked, what on earth would it take to make him happy?

She shuddered to think it. No doubt he wanted a woman who fawned over his every move, who would feed him ice-cold grapes and fetch his slippers in her teeth were he to desire it. Arrogant, entitled man.

Eventually, the limo stopped in front of an ornate pre-war building on Fifth Avenue. A moment later, a uniformed doorman swung the door open and Renzo stepped out before turning and holding out his hand for her. Faith took a deep breath as she gathered her tiny, jeweled purse and tugged her wrap tighter. She thought about refusing his help like she had before, but it was darker now and this was unfamiliar ground. It would not do to land on her face in her finery.

She put her hand in his and let him assist her from the tall SUV. But as her foot hit the pavement, she wobbled in her high heels. She barely had time to lose her balance before Renzo steadied her, a broad hand coming to rest on her waist while the other held her hand firmly.

The hand on her waist seared her. It was like being struck by lightning. They looked at each other for some seconds before he spoke.

"You are full of surprises, Miss Black," Renzo said

softly, his fingers spanning her waist, scorching her
through the silk georgette of her gown.

"Shouldn't you call me Faith?" she asked, her heart
thrumming at both the feel of his hand on her body and
the way he said she was full of surprises. As if he were
pleased.

Oh for God's sake, stop. She could care less what he
thought. Really.

His teeth flashed white in the night. "Of course. *Faith.*
Are you ready to go up? We are expected."

Faith drew in a deep breath. "As ready as I'll ever be."

"You forgot something," he said, his voice sliding across
her nerve endings like a shiver.

Faith blinked up at him, struck anew by the symmetrical beauty of his face. How could a man be so gorgeous?

"What did I forget?" she managed to say without turning into a stammering nitwit. She could feel her face flaming, and she wanted to turn and climb straight back into
the Escalade. And then she wanted to berate herself for
being a ninny.

"As ready as I'll ever be, *Renzo*," he said.

He watched her expectantly, and she realized they
weren't moving until she got it right, no matter how difficult it was for her to think of him as Renzo instead of Mr.
D'Angeli. No matter that it was far safer to think of him
as Mr. D'Angeli. Far easier to maintain her professionalism that way.

But there was no getting around it. He wasn't moving,
and she didn't want to stand on the sidewalk all night.
She'd been lucky there'd been no paparazzi waiting for
him and she didn't feel like tempting fate any further than
she already had.

Not that she was important or her secrets all that earth-shattering—but she'd left her old life behind and she had no wish to revisit the pain and humiliation of it ever again.

She pulled in a breath. "As ready as I'll ever be, *Renzo*."

"*Fabuloso*," he said. "Already, you are perfect."

The Stein's penthouse apartment was magnificent. It took up two levels at the top of the building, and boasted a terrace planted just like a formal English garden. There were trees, arbors, a profusion of rosebushes and even a carpet of grass. Lights strung around the perimeter had the effect of softly illuminating the area and making one believe they were at a garden party. Central Park stretched out below, a dark inky spot in the night bordered by the bright lights of the Upper West Side across the way. If Faith stood near the edge of the terrace and looked left, she could see the Plaza gleaming white while the red taillights of taxis streamed by on Fifth Avenue.

She rarely came into Manhattan. The D'Angeli Motors factory was on Long Island, and she lived in Brooklyn. At the end of the day, she was too tired to venture into the city. And the weekends were her time to read, watch television and catch up on her laundry and housecleaning. She wasn't the sort of girl who had time to pop into the Plaza for afternoon tea.

But now, standing here, she almost wished she was. She could afford that much at least. But a place like the Stein's apartment was another story. This was how the supremely wealthy lived. It was at turns exhilarating and depressing.

She worked long hours to afford what she had and to save up for her own place someday, and other people had manicured grass growing on top of a building in Manhattan. Faith shook her head. Life was very strange sometimes.

She glanced over at Renzo. They'd only been here

twenty minutes, and already she felt that her coming had been a waste of time. He did not need her. He stood nearby, chatting with Robert Stein and a group of gentlemen. They were watching him raptly, laughing and agreeing with something he said, and then toasting him with their glasses held high. A moment later, Stein was turning away at an entreaty from his wife, and Renzo turned to look toward where Faith stood near the terrace wall, a glass of wine in her hand.

There was something electric in his gaze, something that shot straight to the deepest heart of her and twisted an emotion out of her. She took a sip of her wine. How very annoying to not be able to control her response to him. To be exactly like every other woman who couldn't control herself around him.

Except that she could control herself. And she would.

He said something to the men and then he was striding toward her, confident and sure. Until, for the briefest of moments, he seemed to favor his right leg. Faith frowned. A second later, he was moving as gracefully as ever. And yet she was positive he'd been in pain. That was the leg with the pins, the one that had been supposed to end his career several years ago.

"I'm sorry to have left you standing here alone," he said.

Faith shook her head, frowning at the thought his leg might be bothering him. "Not at all. You came here to talk to Mr. Stein. That should take precedence."

He tilted his head as he studied her. It disconcerted her until she wanted to drop her lashes and shield her eyes, but she would not shrink from him. It was not the first time tonight he'd looked at her that way. Each time, she felt as if he were dissecting her and viewing the parts individually. As if he weren't quite certain what to make of her.

Well, she wasn't certain what to make of herself. What

was she doing at a party full of rich people, pretending
to be the date of one of the most handsome and dynamic
men in the world? No one would believe it for a minute.

She didn't. She just wanted to be at home, wrapped in
her fuzzy robe and reading a book. That was believable.

"You are interesting, Faith," Renzo said.

She lifted her chin. She would not be flattered by his
smooth charm. "Not really. I'm just doing my job."

He arched an eyebrow. "Is that what you call it?"

"Yes," she said firmly. "I'm here because you asked me
to be, plus you offered to pay me. It's work."

He looked amused. "And what if I asked you to come
to Italy with me? Would you do it?"

Faith swallowed. Italy? She couldn't pretend that the
thought didn't excite her. She'd never been out of the country before, and she couldn't imagine a more wonderful
place to go. Pasta, pizza, cappuccino. Mmm. It made her
mouth water just to think it.

She'd always believed she would be shuffled to another
of the company's officers once Renzo returned to Europe.
She still believed it. He couldn't really be serious. He had
another factory in Italy, and another office that was no
doubt staffed with an efficient Italian PA.

"That depends," she said, her throat constricting around
the words.

"I need you, Faith. You keep my life together, and I don't
want to live without you."

Faith could only blink. And then she had to suppress
a laugh—because how many women would die to hear
Renzo say those words to them? Of course he meant them
a very different way, but it was still amusing.

"I wish I had a tape recorder," she said, and then bit her
lip when she realized she'd spoken aloud.

He looked perplexed. "Why is this?"

Faith shrugged, laughing. What was the use in denying it? "Because I could probably sell it many times over. I can think of a handful of women who would pay to hear those words from your lips. And I'm sure there are more trailing in your wake. I could retire early."

Renzo laughed. "Ah, *si*, it could be very profitable for you. And yet I hope you will consider my offer to accompany me to Italy."

"You haven't made the offer yet," she said, feeling bold and breathless at the same time.

His smile was turned up full force. "Have I not? Dear Faith, please accompany me to Italy. I will give you a twenty percent raise and cover all your expenses while we are abroad."

Twenty percent. Faith swallowed. "Well, as wonderful as that is, I think you've forgotten something." Because she had to be honest, no matter how much she might like to leap on the offer.

"And what is that?"

"I don't speak Italian. I don't speak anything but English, in fact."

His smile did not dim. "And yet the international language is English. How do you suppose people in Italy converse with people in Germany? No, this is not an issue. Besides, you will learn Italian while you live there."

"I—"

"Renzo, darling, there you are," a cultured female voice called out, interrupting them. "I've been looking everywhere."

Renzo stiffened as he turned toward the owner of the voice. The woman sauntering toward them was a stunning salon-blonde, dressed in a tight-fitting black sheath that showed a mile of tanned leg. Her hair hung long and straight down her back, and her makeup was absolutely

perfect. She wore a fat diamond-drop necklace and matching earrings, and her shoes were gold.

"Lissa," Renzo said. "How nice to see you again."

Lissa's gaze fell to Faith and slid over her with no small
measure of contempt. The look very clearly said *back away*.

Oh puh-leeze. As if Faith were any competition. Still,
she tilted her chin up and stood her ground.

Lissa turned her smile on Renzo. "Do I not get a kiss,
darling? I had thought you Italians were all about the kiss
when greeting friends."

"Of course." Renzo kissed her on both cheeks in the
Italian manner and then turned and put an arm around
Faith. Lissa's eyes narrowed to slits while Faith's entire
body lit up like a firecracker as Renzo pulled her into the
curve of his powerful frame.

This was not what she'd agreed to tonight, and yet in a
way it had been. She was his date.

"Lissa, this is Faith."

Faith held her hand out, surprised it didn't shake when
inside she was trembling so badly. Why, when she didn't
even like him all that much?

Lissa took it after a moment's hesitation. "Very lovely
to meet you," Faith said.

"Yes, lovely." Lissa's tone said it was anything but.
"Renzo, I had hoped to speak with you. Alone," she added,
her smile never wavering.

Renzo's fingers skimmed over Faith's bare arm, his
touch setting off a chain of reactions inside her that ended
with a sharp current of need settling between her thighs.
She'd never felt anything quite like it. And she was furious it was happening now, here, with this man.

Her boss made Casanova look like an amateur, for pity's
sake. She knew it, and yet she responded anyway.

"You may say whatever you wish to say in front of Faith," Renzo countered. "She is completely trustworthy."

Lissa pushed her hair over one shoulder with an indolent gesture. Her eyes sparked. "It can wait," she said tightly. And then she smiled. Faith had the impression of razor-sharp fangs lining the other woman's mouth. "Perhaps a bit later, then."

"Perhaps," Renzo said.

Someone called to her, and Lissa turned and waved. "If you will excuse me, I must mingle."

"Of course," Renzo replied. "Do not let us keep you."

Lissa insisted on kissing Renzo on both cheeks again and held her hand out to Faith, pressing it limply before gliding away in a cloud of malevolence that was quite possibly stronger than her perfume.

"Let me guess," Faith said coolly, moving out of his grasp when the other woman had joined a group of people a few feet away. "She is the reason you needed a date tonight."

"*Si*," Renzo said.

Faith turned to look up at him, exasperated, and just a little hurt. "Honestly, I don't know why you just don't do what you always do and be done with it."

His brows drew together. "What I always do?"

"Oh please, don't act as if you don't know. I've worked for you for six months, and I've yet to see a woman last more than a month with you. You wine them, dine them, give them presents and dump them."

It was bold of her, but she'd had just enough wine to loosen her tongue. To be on the safe side, she deposited the half-finished glass on the terrace wall. If she drank the whole thing, heaven knows what she might say to him.

Renzo grinned. Not at all the effect she'd been going for.

"You forgot one, Faith." She frowned, but he leaned toward her and spoke before she could say anything. "Bed them."

A flash of heat shot through her. Dammit! "Yes, of course. How could I forget that one? Silly me."

She realized she was standing before him with her arms crossed defensively when he put his hands on her shoulders and skimmed them down her arms. "I had no idea you were so outraged by my behavior," he teased.

Faith scoffed as she tried very hard not to react to his skin touching hers. Why didn't she just shove him away? "Outraged? I have no say in anything you choose to do. I am not outraged. It was merely an observation."

He put a finger under her jaw and tipped her chin up. His sharp eyes glittered with some hidden passion that hadn't been there only a moment ago. It shocked her. And intrigued her.

He was so close. Too close, the heat emanating from him enveloping her, making her long to press into him and see just how hot she could feel. Would she burn up in his embrace?

No. No, no, *no*. She would not think of her Italian playboy boss in that way. It wasn't safe. It was irresponsible. *Reckless*.

Faith did not do reckless. The one time she had, it had cost her far more than she could have ever dreamed. She was finished with reckless.

"But you disapprove," Renzo said.

"Not this time." And she almost meant it, except for the fact it would mean Renzo would actually sleep with that obnoxious woman. Though, on the other hand, the woman would pay for it in the end when Renzo dumped her. Faith might enjoy shopping for that parting gift. "Go for it."

He laughed. "And what makes you think I have not already? That she just doesn't understand I no longer want her?"

It was a valid point, but she knew better because she'd witnessed the fallout too many times. The tears, the desperate phone calls, the attempts to sneak past her and into his office in order to plead for another chance. Women could be, she'd decided, awfully pitiful sometimes. She wanted to tell them to get some dignity, to stop begging and go on with their lives. Men like Renzo were immune to histrionics.

"Because a woman who has been subjected to the D'Angeli treatment is usually angry with you. She wasn't. She wants you, and pretty badly I'd say."

The look in his eyes was sharp. He moved a step closer and she shuddered involuntarily. "What are you doing?" she asked.

"Nothing," he said, much too innocently. "I like the way you talk, Faith. It sounds like sweet syrup, all long and drawn out as if you had all day to speak. Not like the women in New York."

"That's because I'm from Georgia. It's hot there. We talk slow and walk slow and, well, do a lot of things slow." My God, she was babbling. To her urbane, gorgeous boss. Where was her dignity?

One of Renzo's dark eyebrows arched. "Really? I can imagine that some things are done best when done slowly. How wise you people from Georgia are."

Her heart was slamming into her ribs and a fine sheen of moisture was rising in the valley between her breasts. "I sound no different now than I have for the past six months. I can't imagine how you haven't noticed it before."

He took another step and she backed up, found herself against the wall of the terrace where it curved inward. He put a hand on the wall beside her, trapping her as his other hand came up and caressed her jaw.

It was electrifying.

"I have been wondering this myself," he said. "You have hidden yourself well, Faith."

Her body hummed with electricity that she feared would scorch her if it continued for much longer. "I've hidden nothing. I've come to work every day and sat at a desk not ten feet from your office door. I've brought you coffee, papers. I've fielded phone calls and given you reports. And I've gone shopping for those goodbye presents for your women—"

"Ah," he said softly, "you *are* offended."

"No," she replied. But then, because she couldn't help it, she added, "Though I think you should shop for your own presents."

Renzo laughed. "Perhaps you are correct, and yet you always choose the nicest things. How can I compete?"

"By employing a full-time personal shopper?"

His gaze dropped to her mouth for a moment and she sucked in a breath, trying to calm her racing heart. He hadn't backed away, hadn't taken his hand from her cheek in all this time they'd been talking. The sharp ache throbbing inside her was nearly unbearable.

And unfathomable.

"You have lovely eyes," he said. "Why do you hide them behind those hideous glasses all day long?"

She stiffened. "They're reading glasses. I need them to do my job." A different kind of heat scorched her now.

Someone laughed nearby, and then Lissa's voice drifted over the others. "So plain and unattractive. Honestly, I can't see what he sees in her. Must be an Italian thing."

Time seemed to stand still for a moment, hovering in the air above Faith's head, threatening her with old humiliations and hurts. And then it drifted down over her, covering her in feelings she would rather forget.

She told herself not to care, but she did anyway. It hurt, being the center of negative attention. Though nothing Lissa said could come close to what Faith had gone through in the past when Jason had betrayed her trust, she was surprised to realize that it still had the power to hurt her.

For a moment, she was back in high school. Hearing the taunts, the snickers, the innuendos. Feeling the anger, the urge to lash out, the urge to escape.

Renzo's jaw tightened. "I'm sorry, Faith."

"It's nothing," she said lightly, drawing on hard-won reserves of strength. "She's just jealous." But moisture swam in her eyes and her throat ached with the effort not to let any tears fall. She thought that she'd learned how to deal with this eight years ago, but she'd been wrong. You never got over people pointing their fingers and laughing at you.

"We will go now," Renzo said, his hands on her shoulders once more, this time imparting comfort rather than setting her on edge.

"No!" Faith swallowed the lump in her throat. She would not run. Not this time. "No, that's exactly what she wants. Besides, have you got what you came here for tonight?"

He'd spent a few minutes with Robert Stein, but it had been in the company of others. And she was fairly certain he'd not talked business upon first arriving. No doubt he'd been hoping to broach that subject a bit later.

He frowned. "That is unimportant."

Impulsively, she put a hand on his chest. The fabric of his tuxedo was smooth, cool, but beneath it his body was hard and hot. She knew he was in excellent shape considering that he was a top Grand Prix rider—not to mention she'd saved the heat-inducing magazine ad where he'd posed in his leathers with the zipper opened to his navel.

She'd been unable to deny how sexy he was in that ad, even if she did think him heartless when it came to women. The magazine had gone into her keeper pile, much to her dismay.

Still, after all that, she was unprepared for how his body felt beneath her hand.

Power and leashed strength waiting for the right instant to explode into action. At the moment, however, he seemed very still beneath her touch, nothing but the beat of his heart vibrating against her palm. It was almost as if he was purposely holding himself still.

Faith forced herself to focus. "Please, Renzo, the Viper is important to you. Talk with Mr. Stein. Don't worry about me. I can handle myself."

She'd learned how after a trial by fire she would never forget.

His fingers wrapped around hers where they rested on his tuxedo. He lifted her hand to his lips and pressed a kiss there that sent a shudder rocketing down her spine.

"You are quite remarkable, Faith," he said softly.

"Hardly," she replied. She needed to put distance between them, now more than ever. She didn't like this hot, achy feeling he called up inside her. It could come to no good for her. Even if he were interested in a plain girl like her, she had a lot more to lose than his usual women. Unlike the others, she'd find herself brokenhearted *and* jobless once he decided to dump her, were she foolish enough to give in to this silliness inside. "I'm thinking of my bottom line. If the Viper succeeds, then I can ask for an even bigger raise."

Renzo threw back his head and laughed. "Indeed. Then come with me, *cara*."

And, twining his fingers in hers, he led her into the center of the garden party.

CHAPTER THREE

RENZO was in a good mood. Aside from Lissa Stein's behavior—and the way his leg now throbbed after so much time standing on it—it had been a good evening. Stein had expressed interest in building custom tires for the Viper, and an acute interest in an exclusive partnership with D'Angeli Motors, should the Viper prove a success during the time trials next month in Italy. The bike wasn't quite ready yet, but Renzo had high hopes they'd be able to begin training for the MotoGP season soon.

But, more interestingly, he was very much intrigued by the woman sitting beside him in the limousine. He'd kept her close for the rest of the evening, ushering her through the gathering like a prized possession. Lissa Stein had stayed far away, *grazie a Dio*.

While that had been his priority in bringing Faith tonight, he'd found that he rather enjoyed having her near. She made no demands. She did not simper or whine or pout. In fact, she seemed quite prickly, and she'd taken him to task over the women in his life. Rather than finding it impertinent, he'd been amused.

She might bristle like a porcupine, but he couldn't help noticing that she'd shivered and blushed when he'd touched her. And that it seemed to infuriate her that she had.

When he'd backed her against the terrace wall and put

his hand on her cheek, he'd had every intention of kissing her even though he knew he should not. He'd never yet committed the sin of making love to a personal assistant, and he wasn't sure he wanted to cross that line now. But he *had* wanted to taste her. Just for an instant.

He still wasn't certain why. Faith Black was not a gorgeous model, but she had some indefinable quality about her that he couldn't quite pinpoint. She was strong, but also vulnerable. She'd experienced pain in her life, but that pain hadn't defeated her. He'd seen it in her eyes when Lissa had made those hurtful comments. He'd wanted to defend her, but she hadn't needed defending.

"I have not forgotten that you did not answer me about Italy," he said into the silence.

The interior of the car was dark, other than the lights from the street that shone inside as they drove back toward Brooklyn. One of Faith's earrings caught the light as she turned her head toward him.

"I've been thinking about it," she said.

"And what have you been thinking?"

"You didn't tell me how it would work once I got there. Where would I live? Would I need a car? I haven't driven in years, and I'm not sure I'd feel comfortable relearning that skill in a foreign country. It's not that I can't drive," she hurried on, "but since I've lived in New York, it's been unnecessary."

She sounded somewhat breathless, he noted, as if she were nervous and trying to hide it. Interesting.

"I have a very large house, *cara*. You would stay with me. And there is no need to drive, as you will travel with me wherever I go."

Wherever he went? Renzo surprised himself with the statement, but *si*, it made the most sense. How could she organize his appointments if she did not accompany him?

"I'm not sure I could do that," she said very quietly.

"Why not?" He sounded perplexed. Because he *was* perplexed.

"Because at least I have weekends off now. I have my own life, you know. It does not revolve around you twenty-four hours a day. And it sounds like it would in Italy."

A sudden thought occurred to him. Perhaps it should have occurred to him before, but the simple fact was that it hadn't. "Do you have a boyfriend, Faith? Someone you do not wish to leave behind?"

He knew what he wanted the answer to be, but he had no idea what she would say. If she would ruin his good mood by giving him a different answer than he desired.

"No, no boyfriend," she said.

A sliver of relief slid through him at her soft words. Not that he cared if she had a boyfriend, of course. But it would make it much easier if she did not.

"Any pets?"

"No. No pets. I had a cat, but he died last year."

"I'm sorry."

She shrugged, as if she were trying to say it was nothing. And yet he wasn't fooled. He could hear the sadness in her voice. "It's fine. He was old and it was his time. I wanted to get a kitten, but they need so much attention. Well, any cat does, really, and I work a lot so…"

Her voice trailed off and he found himself feeling somewhat guilty, as if he was at fault because she hadn't gotten another cat. He did work long hours, and sometimes she stayed behind, too, not leaving the office until after seven or eight in the evening.

No, a cat would not like that. Neither would a boyfriend.

She shrugged again. "I'm sorry. You didn't really want to know all that. I'm babbling."

"I've never heard you babble, Faith. I would hardly classify this as babbling." He knew babbling. Katie had been a babbler. He'd found it somewhat annoying that she couldn't ever stop talking, but he'd tried to keep her mouth too occupied to talk whenever they were together.

Renzo frowned. What had he ever seen in Katie? Besides the perfect body, of course? She'd been so shallow, so self-absorbed. Why had he surrounded himself with that?

"Well, I'm babbling now. My mom would say I—"

He heard her indrawn breath. "Would say what?" he prodded when she didn't continue.

"Nothing. It's nothing." She'd folded her hands on her lap again, and he found himself wanting to take one of her soft hands in his and rub circles in her palm the way he'd done before. Just to feel that tremor slide through her.

"You can tell me," he said.

"I'd rather not."

She sounded so prim, so controlled. It made him wonder. How had she worked for him for six months and he didn't know anything about her? She didn't seem to want to talk about her past. And though he wanted to command her to tell him what she'd been about to say, he could hardly do so. It wasn't like he enjoyed talking about his past—his family—either.

His mother was a good woman who'd worked hard all her life, but he was still somewhat embarrassed by his origins. He shouldn't be, but he was. Not because of her, but because of the Conte de Lucano. From the moment he'd learned who his father was when he was eight years old, the one time the man had come to see them and threatened his mother if she dared tell anyone who had fathered her child, he'd felt inferior. Damaged. Like garbage tossed on a scrap heap.

For all he knew, Faith felt the same. "You do not like talking about your family," he said.

She sighed. "No, I don't like talking about them. I left years ago and I'm never going back."

It was the closest thing to a vow he'd ever heard her utter. She said it with such conviction. Such bitterness.

Such passion.

Renzo felt a jolt of awareness curl through him. *Maledizione,* was he mad? She was his PA, and though he didn't quite understand where this sudden attraction to her sprang from, she was most definitely off-limits. She had to be. He needed to concentrate on the Viper, and he needed his efficient PA at his side, taking care of the business side of his life while he rode the hell out of the motorcycle and worked on the adjustments to the design. If he crossed the line with her, he could endanger everything—in so much as she might leave and he'd have to train a new PA when he did not have the time.

No, Renzo could not afford to endanger anything right now when time was critical. When Niccolo Gavretti was just waiting to find a weakness he could exploit in his quest to destroy Renzo and D'Angeli Motors. He should have crushed Niccolo when he'd had the chance, but he'd been sentimental. *Idiot.*

"I don't suppose you care to tell me why," he said, more than a little curious about what could make quiet, calm Faith Black run away from home.

Her head moved, the lights shining off her golden hair as she shook it. "Some families don't get along," she said. "Let's just leave it at that."

He could only stare. He'd thought her sweet, harmless, and here she was made of steel and wrapped in velvet. Faith did not speak to her family. It was a revelation, and he burned with curiosity as to why. He spoke to his mother and sister regularly, couldn't imagine not speaking to them. But here was this quiet girl telling him with such vehemence that she'd cut herself off from everyone in her life.

It stunned him. This was a woman with unsuspected depths. A woman who'd worked for him for six months, and he'd never once realized there was more to her than the face she presented him with every day.

The car pulled to a stop in front of her apartment building. He thought she might make a dash for it, but she waited for Stefan to come around and open the door. Renzo stepped out onto the pavement, his leg throbbing so badly now that he knew he would need a pain pill when he got home. At least, mercifully, the damn thing would make him sleep.

"You don't have to see me up," Faith said as he started toward the building door.

He turned toward her, saw the worry lines bracketing her mouth, and knew that she'd seen through him. For some reason, that made him angry.

"I do," he said shortly, his tone brooking no argument. A part of him was saying he was a fool, but the other part— the prideful, stubborn part—insisted he could still do any damn thing he wanted to do. It was simply an issue of mind over matter. If he couldn't conquer the little things, like stairs, how could he conquer the big things, like riding the Viper on the Grand Prix circuit?

Faith turned away in a huff and walked to the door. He followed her. She used her key to get inside the building, and then they were moving toward the stairs. She took her time, saying her high heels were bothering her, but he suspected she did it for him.

His leg cramped as he climbed the two flights, but then they were in the hall and standing before her door. Pain spiked into his leg then, radiating through his entire body so that he leaned against the wall, certain he wouldn't be moving for at least five minutes. *Per Dio.*

Faith unlocked her door and turned, a little gasp escaping her when she saw him standing there. "Renzo? Are you okay?"

"*Si,* of course," he said, but his voice sounded as if he were gritting his teeth. Which he was, he realized a moment later.

Faith didn't hesitate. She looped her arm in his. "Come in and sit down. Let me massage it for you."

Now why, in the midst of his pain, did that thought make his libido kick into gear?

"I'll be fine in a few moments. Just let me stand here." It wasn't an admission he'd wanted to make, but he wasn't so stubborn as to deny the truth when she could clearly see it.

She frowned up at him. "I had a roommate who was a massage therapist, and she taught me some things. I'm not a professional, but I can try to ease the cramp."

"It will go away in a moment."

Her expression said she didn't believe it for a minute. "I can massage it or you can stand here. Whichever you prefer. But know this. My feet hurt and I'm going inside and sitting down, with or without you."

He swore softly in Italian, but he let her help him into the cramped living space of her apartment. He didn't even bother trying to hide the limp this time. What was the point?

She eased him down on her sofa and then hastily moved magazines from her coffee table before bending to pick his foot up and prop it on the table. Renzo leaned his head back and closed his eyes as pain throbbed into his body.

"You shouldn't have stood on it so long tonight," Faith said.

"This rarely happens," he replied automatically, though

it was a lie. In truth it happened too often of late. And what if it happened on the track? He'd been asking himself that for months now. The consequences could be disastrous. He knew what it was like to wipe out at two hundred miles an hour. Knew how lucky he'd been to wake up from the accident with pins in his leg and his head intact.

"Yes, well, you should still think of it and take opportunities to rest the leg when you can." Faith sank down onto the couch beside him, her body pressing against his as she leaned over him and put her small hands on his thigh.

Renzo swallowed. Hard. He was in pain, yes, but he wasn't dead. His body wanted to respond to the feel of her hands pressing into him, but he refused to allow it. His senses were filled with her—with the sweet scent of her, the tactile pressure of her hands on his body, the sound of her breath and her voice. With his eyes closed, he didn't have to ask himself what it was about her. He could *feel* what it was, though he'd be damned if he could name it.

"The muscles are so tight," she said. "It would be much better if you took your pants off."

Renzo couldn't help but laugh, though the sound was nothing like his usual laugh. He wasn't quite sure if it was strained from the pain of his leg or the pain of fighting with himself not to reach for her. "*Cara*, you surprise me."

"That's not what I meant," she said, sounding all prickly and cool.

Renzo opened his eyes. She was looking at his leg, concentrating on massaging it, but a red flush had spread over her cheeks. Her face in profile was lovelier than he'd imagined. He couldn't stop himself from lifting his hand. From sliding his finger across her soft cheek.

"And yet I could almost wish you did," he said, and her head came up, her green eyes so wide and innocent. Innocent? He wasn't sure where he'd gotten that thought from.

"Are you flirting with me, Mr. D'Angeli?"

"Not if you prefer I didn't," he told her truthfully, disappointed that she'd retreated behind formality once more.

Her gaze dropped again. Her fingers kneaded his knotted muscles. It hurt, and yet he knew she was loosening them at the same time.

"That is exactly what I prefer," she said. "You *are* charming, but your charm is misdirected on me."

His brows drew together. She was bent over him, her head bowed, her cleavage frustratingly covered—and yet he would have sworn he felt the spark between them, too.

"Is it?" he asked, aggravated that she was so distant and formal.

"The last thing you need is another woman puffing up your already-outrageous ego," she stated firmly. "So, if you don't mind, while I am certain you could charm the panties off a nun, I'd prefer if you didn't attempt it on me."

Her heart thudded in her ears. Faith couldn't believe she'd actually said that to him. She was not unaffected by his male beauty, no matter how she protested otherwise. But he didn't need to know that, did he?

Except he wasn't a stupid man. When he'd touched her, she'd felt the blush bloom across her cheeks. Surely he'd seen it. Just as he'd no doubt heard the breathy note in her voice when she'd asked if he was flirting with her.

She'd denied she was affected, but it was a lie. What living, breathing woman wouldn't be attracted to this man?

Faith wanted to snort in disgust. Really, *she* should be the woman who wasn't because she'd watched him go through at least five girlfriends since she'd worked for him. Not only that, but she'd also seen the tabloid reports on his notorious love-them-and-leave-them lifestyle. How could she ever find a man like him attractive?

And yet she did.

"I don't believe I've ever charmed a nun," he said, his voice containing a hint of steel beneath the silk. "I only charm those who wish to be charmed."

"Then I'll consider myself safe." The tops of her ears burned.

"For now," he said.

Faith tried to concentrate on the ropes of muscle beneath her hands. It would be so much easier if she could touch his skin instead of his trousers, but this was definitely safer. Seeing his body, touching his skin—it made curls of heat sizzle into her just thinking of it. Even now, though there was fabric between her skin and his, it wasn't quite enough to block the sensuality of touching him.

Concentrate.

Faith pressed her thumbs into the muscle and worked at the knots. She wasn't a true massage therapist, but she'd thought she could help him by using a couple of the things that Elaine had taught her before moving back to Ohio.

What else could she do? She couldn't let him stand out there in the hall, and she couldn't let him go back downstairs when he was in such pain.

"Should I go down and tell Stefan what's happened?" she asked, suddenly remembering the uniformed man they'd left on the street.

"I'll call." Renzo took his phone out of his pocket.

"He can come up, if you like."

Renzo's eyes were flat. "No, that is not necessary."

Faith supposed Stefan was quite used to waiting outside women's apartments. The thought did not cheer her. Would the man think his boss was up here getting cozy with her? Did she care?

Renzo made the call, told Stefan to go home while Faith tried not to swallow her tongue, and then hung up and gave her an even look.

"Don't look so worried," he told her. "I'll take a taxi home."

She bit the inside of her cheek and told herself it didn't matter if Stefan thought Renzo was spending the night with her. It was getting late and Stefan would want to return home, so it was kind of Renzo not to make him wait.

"Is this helping at all?" she asked, still pressing her thumbs into his thigh muscle.

"*Si*, I think so."

"How long has this been going on, Mr. D'Angeli?"

His icy blue eyes glittered. "I refuse to discuss this with you unless you call me Renzo."

Faith's cheeks heated. "I had thought it best if we go back to the way things were before the party tonight."

Because she needed to put distance between them. She needed to remember that he was her boss, and not a man she could ever know more personally.

"And I disagree. If you wish to know about my leg, Faith, you will address me the way I have asked you to. It seems a bit ridiculous to call me Mr. D'Angeli considering where your hands are, yes?"

She barely resisted the urge to pinch him. "If this were a spa, I highly doubt you'd be asking the technician to call you Renzo."

He arched an eyebrow. "Depends on how attractive she was, I imagine."

"You're incorrigible," she said.

"And possessed of an outrageous ego, I understand."

Faith couldn't help but laugh. "Oh dear. I'm sorry I said that." It might be true, but she shouldn't have said it. One evening pretending to be his date didn't give her a license to insult him. He was still her boss when everything was said and done.

"You aren't sorry at all. And I don't mind." He shrugged. "Perhaps it is true."

"Will you tell me about your leg now?"

"Will you agree to call me Renzo?"

What else could she say? "Yes."

"*Bene*." He sighed. "It happens more lately than it used to. The doctors told me I would never walk without a limp, that I would always need a cane—but I proved them wrong. Except," he said with a hint of bitterness in his voice, "that it seems as if my victory was only temporary."

She stopped rubbing for half a second, her fingers going limp at the thought of this proud man needing a cane once more. "There is nothing that can be done?"

"Probably not. But I will not give in just yet." He leaned toward her then, took her chin in his fingers and forced her to look at him. "No one can know about this, Faith. It's very important that no one knows."

She could only blink at him. "I don't see how you can keep it a secret if something like this happens again."

He released her and sat back again. "I won't let it happen."

"That didn't work so well for you tonight, did it?" She was growing angry, and not because he was stubborn, but because he frightened her. She knew where this conviction sprang from, knew what he did not say. The Viper. The Grand Prix circuit. Though he had a racing team, he didn't feel anyone else could ride the bike to victory just yet. It was personal to him, though she did not quite know why.

The arrogant man intended to risk his neck on the track and to hell with everything else. It infuriated her.

She got to her feet, her entire body trembling with energy. She needed to move, needed to do something, or she might explode. *Why did she care?*

"Do you want something to drink?"

He was watching her carefully. "A brandy would be nice."

She wanted to laugh, but she did not. "I'm sorry, but this isn't the Ritz. I don't have a liquor cabinet. I may have some vodka, though."

Elaine had liked vodka and Faith was pretty sure she'd left half a bottle behind.

"And tonic water," she added. "I know I have that."

"Vodka and tonic would be fine," he said. Faith turned and fled to the kitchen. She found the vodka shoved in the back of a cabinet. Then she filled a glass with ice, added some vodka and poured tonic water on top. For good measure, she made another for herself. She wasn't much of a drinker, but she had the feeling she needed something to take the edge off.

This night had been strange, to say the least.

Renzo was sitting where she'd left him, his leg still propped up, his head leaning back against the sofa cushion. His eyes were closed, and she took a moment to admire the symmetrical beauty of his face. His nose was long and lean, his cheekbones high, his lips full and firm. He had a mouth made to kiss, she thought. His top lip dipped in the center, just slightly, and she found herself wanting to nibble on that sexy little dip.

It was a sensual mouth. A cruel mouth. A mouth she wanted on hers even though she knew better. Just for a moment. Just so she could see for herself what made all those women so willing to put up with this man.

His eyes snapped open, then went unerringly to her face. The heat she saw there was unmistakable. It nearly fixed her feet to the spot, but she forced herself to move as if nothing was any different. As if they were still Miss Black and Mr. D'Angeli, and this was simply a morning at the office and she was taking him coffee.

She crossed the distance between them and held out the drink. "*Grazie,*" he said, taking it from her and sitting it on the table beside him.

She set her own drink down and turned back to him, prepared to ask if he wanted her to continue rubbing his leg. But the look in his eyes scorched her.

Renzo reached up and took her hand in his. Her skin sizzled as fire snaked through her.

"You feel it, too," he said. "I know you do."

Faith could not speak. She did feel it, whatever *it* was. And she didn't like it. It made her achy and jumpy and worried. He was the wrong man, the man who could destroy her present just as Jason Moore had destroyed her past.

With one tug, he pulled her down onto his lap, his arms going around her to cradle her close. "Renzo," she started to protest, but he bent and fitted his gorgeous mouth to hers, silencing her.

CHAPTER FOUR

So many sensations crashed through Faith at once: confusion, fear, lust, passion, joy. She wanted to slide her arms around his neck, arch into him and beg him to show her what no man ever had before.

And she wanted to shove away from him, put as much distance between them as possible. She wanted him to go. And she wanted him to stay.

His mouth on hers was firm, sensual, demanding. His tongue slid across the seam of her lips, enticing her, entreating her. She was determined not to give in to the invitation, but he caressed her cheek and she gasped. His tongue slipped inside her mouth, stroked against hers.

It was, in its own way, heaven. Her heart hammered so hard in her ears that she could hear nothing else.

Faith made a sound, realized it was a moan. It was a needy sound from deep in her throat, the kind of sound that invited a man to continue, to take it further.

No! No, no, no. That was not at all what she wanted. She wanted it to stop—

And yet she made no move to stop it. In fact, she shivered in his embrace at the thought of more. The truth was that Renzo D'Angeli kissed like he'd been born to do so. His mouth moved over hers, fitted to hers, coaxed hers.

And she gave, gave as much as she was able, gave more than she thought she could.

She meant to push him away, but she wound her arms around his neck instead, let the hot sensations roll over her. She was electric, incandescent, her body sparking and tightening in ways she'd not thought possible. This was what drew the women, then. *This.*

A moment later she tilted, and then the world was shifting as he pressed her back onto the couch, his hard strong body pressing into hers. Panic shot through her. It suddenly reminded her of another time, another place, when she was young and innocent and thought she was in love. Jason had pressed her onto her parents' couch just like this, his body rubbing hers almost painfully, his hands grasping and groping beneath her dress.

Renzo did nothing of the sort, and yet Faith couldn't get the images out of her head. The fear, the panic. *A good girl wouldn't do such a thing, Faith. A good girl keeps her body sacred until she enters into the bonds of matrimony.*

It was her father talking, but she suddenly couldn't make the sainted Reverend Winston go away. And she couldn't allow that ugliness to ruin whatever beautiful feeling was crashing through her because of Renzo.

She put her hands on Renzo's shoulders and pushed. He lifted his head, a question in his blue eyes, and Faith took the opportunity to scramble out from under him. She fell onto the floor in a tangle of fabric, then shoved herself upright and retreated across the room.

Renzo stood, his features dark and alarmed. "Faith?"

Faith wrapped her arms around her body. "I'm sorry, but that was a mistake. I didn't mean for it to go that far, so please just forget it happened."

He looked stormy, and so sexy she wanted to weep. Had

that gorgeous, gorgeous man really been kissing her? Little Faith Louise Winston of all damn people?

"Forget?" he asked dangerously. "I hardly think that is possible, Faith."

"It was a mistake," she said. "I work for you, and to-morrow I'll be at the office like always, and you'll be there doing what you always do, and it will be so awkward that I'll want to scream. But I won't. And you'll find a new girlfriend soon, and then you can forget about kissing me."

He shoved his hand through his hair, muttering in Italian, and then picked up his vodka and tonic and drained it. "Why would I want to forget it, Faith?"

"Because I'm nothing special," she said. Good Lord, was the man dense?

"Don't talk like that," he commanded, his eyes flashing, and she laughed nervously.

"Don't worry. I don't think I'm awful or anything. I *am* special, but in my world. Not in yours. You wouldn't even be here if you hadn't dumped Katie Palmer today."

"Katie Palmer has nothing to do with this," he growled.

"But she does," Faith said, hoping she sounded as cool and logical as she was trying so hard to be. She'd been kissing Lorenzo D'Angeli, motorcycle magnate, Grand Prix bad boy, right here in her humble little living room. If he weren't still standing there in all his magnificently male glory, she'd think she was making the whole thing up. That the vodka and tonic she hadn't even taken a sip of had gone to her head and made her hallucinate. "Katie Palmer is the kind of woman you prefer. All your girlfriends have looked like some version of her, you know."

His gaze narrowed, but she tumbled on recklessly. "Tall, leggy, effortlessly beautiful, with long dark hair and per-fect makeup and size zero bodies that could really probably use a hamburger or two a bit more often…" She cleared her throat, waved a hand down her body. "As you can see, I am none of those things. I'm short, curvy and not in the least bit effortlessly beautiful. And I like to eat. Pasta, hamburgers, the occasional French fry. No, you should really go find that Lissa woman and make her your next fling."

He looked utterly furious. "*Santo cielo,* I am not arguing with you over this." He took his phone from his pocket. "Perhaps you are correct. Lissa would certainly not argue with me when I wanted to kiss her."

"Not many women would," Faith said, stung in spite of everything she'd said to push him away.

"But you did." He made a call to a taxi company while she stood there feeling miserable, her heart squeezing tight as she wondered if she'd made a mistake.

Of course she hadn't. He was her boss!

"I need our relationship to be professional," she said when he finished his call, as much to convince herself as him. "I like my job and I don't want to feel uncomfortable there."

Renzo waved a hand as if it were nothing. Which, to him, it probably was. Women came and went with alarming regularity in his life. What was one more?

Indeed, his fury with her seemed forgotten as he moved toward the door with only the barest trace of a limp. "It never happened, Faith. Thank you for the massage, and for the drink. I will see you in the office tomorrow."

And then he walked out and left her standing there, her lips still tingling and her body aching with thwarted desire. Either she was the bravest woman in the world, or the biggest fool to send him away.

The problem was that she wasn't quite sure which.

Renzo got into the office early the next morning. Faith had not yet arrived when he walked past her desk and into his office with the tall windows and custom decor. Low-slung Italian leather couches faced each other in front of his desk, and he dropped onto one of them to read the reports that were sitting on the table there.

The Viper was nearly ready to take to Italy. The thought should fill him with triumph, and yet it only made him worry about what else might go wrong. He'd taken a pain pill last night, and this morning he felt perfectly fine—but when was the next time his leg would give out? And what would his rivals do if they learned he was not at his best? Niccolo Gavretti was looking for a chance to cream him. If his biggest rival knew about his weakness, he would exploit it whenever and however possible.

And then there was Faith. Renzo rubbed his temples for a moment and then dropped the reports. Where had his world-renowned cool gone last night when he'd needed it? He'd succumbed to the temptation to kiss her because she'd bent over him and her scent had driven him insane. He'd wanted just a taste. One brief taste, to see if he was losing his mind in lusting after his PA, or if there was something more beneath that buttoned-up surface.

He could still remember the utter shock he'd felt when his mouth touched hers. The lightning bolt of excitement that had rocketed through him with the same force as a fast ride on a fast track. There was nothing more exhilarating than opening up the throttle and giving the bike gas.

But kissing Faith had compared to that feeling. He'd wanted her. His body had gone from zero to two hundred plus in a matter of seconds. Even thinking of it now made him hard.

He knew when a woman wanted him, and she definitely had. And he'd had every intention of taking advantage of the chemistry between them at that moment. He'd been unable to stop himself from pressing her back on the couch when she'd kissed him with such fervor.

She was hot and sweet and more innocent than she seemed. She'd kissed him with all the finesse of a rank amateur, and yet it had done nothing but heat his blood. He usually liked his women polished and experienced, but Faith had managed to make him forget his preferences.

He'd wanted her and damn the consequences of sleeping with his PA. Hell, he still wanted her. He'd told her the kiss was forgotten, but he had forgotten nothing.

There was a knock on his door and he glanced at his watch. Eight o'clock on the dot, which meant it was probably Faith arriving. "Enter," he said, standing up and crossing to his desk.

The door slid open and Faith stood there in a boxy black suit, short heels, and with her hair scraped back on her head as always. "I wasn't sure if you were here," she said briskly. "Would you like coffee, Mr. D'Angeli?"

A trickle of annoyance filtered through him. "*Si,* that would be good, thank you."

She turned away.

"Faith," he called, and she stopped, pivoted to face him again.

"Yes sir?"

The formality grated on him, but he knew she did it to keep him at a distance. He wanted to tell her to take her hair down. To take off that ridiculous boxy jacket and unbutton her blouse to show some cleavage. To come over and wrap her arms around him so he could fit her body to his and kiss her thoroughly.

He would, of course, say none of those things. Another woman would smile and pout and do exactly what he wanted. But not Faith. If he said those things to her, she would slay him with a cold stare. And then she would walk out of his office and he'd be lucky if she ever came back.

"We're leaving for Italy in a week. Please make arrangements."

Her jaw dropped and for a moment he thought she would refuse. He waited for it, wondered how he would command her to go once she'd turned him down. Because he wanted her there with him. Because, *maledizione*, he *wanted* her. She intrigued him like no one else with her hidden beauty and prickly demeanor.

And her secrets. He wanted to know her secrets. What had made sweet Faith turn her back on her family?

Color bloomed on her cheeks, brought life and sparkle to her glorious eyes. She hesitated for a long minute. "Yes sir," she said. "I will."

Faith had never been outside of the United States before. She had her passport, because it had been required when she'd started working for D'Angeli Motors, but she'd never actually thought she would have reason to use it.

Now, as she stood in her apartment and looked around to make sure she'd forgotten nothing, she could hardly believe she was going. Renzo hadn't been able to tell her how long they would be gone, but he'd told her to continue to pay her rent here if it made her comfortable since she would be provided housing in Italy at no extra charge.

In his house. Faith gulped. She would be living in his house, a stone's throw away from him, for twenty-four hours a day. Why had she agreed to go? How could she live with him, as an employee, and watch him go about his life as if nothing had ever happened between the two of them? He had already forgotten it, as he'd assured her he would, while she could think of little else.

But that wasn't the worst of it. The worst was that she

imagined he would most certainly entertain women from time to time. In the same house she'd be living in. As an employee.

Faith made a noise that sounded suspiciously like a cry of distress. She'd meant to refuse to go. She'd meant to tell him that she couldn't go to Italy and could she please have a transfer to another office, but she'd stood there and looked at his handsome face, at the mouth she'd been kissing only hours earlier, and felt all her resolve crumble into nothing.

She'd said yes, just like some besotted female. She was furious with herself over it. For hours, she'd debated going back in there and telling him no, telling him she'd made a mistake and she wanted to stay right here, thank you very much.

But she hadn't. And now a car was waiting to take her to JFK for the flight to Italy. She took one last look around, and then locked the door behind her and headed down to the street. The driver had already taken her luggage down, so that when she emerged from the building, he popped out of the car and came around to open her door.

She slid into the plush interior of the black town car and belted herself in for the ride. It took nearly an hour in traffic to reach the airport, but once there she was ushered onto a huge Boeing business jet that belonged to D'Angeli Motors.

The interior was nothing like any plane she'd ever been on. She'd had no occasion to board the company's international jet before, but now she gaped at the sumptuous interior. Renzo was a wealthy man indeed if he could afford all this. Rich wood grains, buttery leather chairs and couches, a bar, televisions and custom carpeting that had the D'Angeli Motors logo woven into it. It was all so stunning, and it only served to remind her of how ridiculous it was to think he'd actually wanted her the night of the party. She was not the sort of sophisticated woman who matched this lifestyle.

In fact, she'd been thinking of other plane trips she'd taken in the past and she'd dressed for comfort with the typical economy class seating in mind. She wore stretchy jeans, a hooded sweatshirt and tennis shoes she could slip on and off without untying. In her carry-on backpack, she had a couple of books, an ereader, a music player and headphones, along with a few power bars and a bottle of water. She even had a travel pillow, which seemed silly since she was positive this jet was probably equipped with real pillows and blankets.

A sophisticated woman would have arrived wearing the latest fashions and carrying matching luggage—Louis Vuitton, no doubt—instead of dressed like a refugee and carrying snacks.

She was embarrassed suddenly, and it made her uncomfortable. She knew what it was like to feel like an outsider, like an idiot, and though wearing the wrong clothing and failing to be sophisticated didn't compare to what had happened before, the shame and anger were similar.

She felt stupid, useless, and she stood and clenched her fingers into fists, digging her nails into her palms. She'd left naive Faith Winston behind when she'd left home and changed her name, but that Faith sometimes crept up on her and made her feel as if she'd escaped nothing after all. As if she were still the preacher's daughter who'd been so stupid as to send a scandalous picture to a boy.

"Ah, Faith," Renzo said, and she looked up to see him standing just inside the entrance to the main cabin and smiling at her. She swallowed at the sight of him. His sharp blue eyes raked over her, appraising her—and no doubt found her lacking. He was dressed for comfort, too, she noted, but his jeans were designer labeled, and the soft cotton shirt he wore unbuttoned over a navy D'Angeli Motors T-shirt was probably hand woven by cloistered virgins or some such.

Because, if any man could afford such a thing, it would be Renzo.

He came forward and took her arm, leading her back toward the cabin he'd been in. "You look lovely," he said in her ear as he stopped just short of the entry.

Fire leaped along her nerve endings. "No, not really," she blurted, confusion and fear breaking through the surface of her calm.

His eyes dropped over her again. "And I say you do." He gave her arm a squeeze and then led her into the room he'd come from.

Two men sat at a table, papers spread out across the surface, but they stood as she entered the room with Renzo. She recognized them as two of the engineers on the project. "You have met Bill and Sergio before, have you not?" Renzo said, gesturing to the two men.

"I've met them, yes," she said, shaking hands with each man in turn. They were polite, but she was certain they were curious. Renzo had an entire staff at his Italian headquarters. Could he really not find a PA who kept his appointments straight?

Renzo put a hand on the small of her back. It was a possessive move, a familiar move, though it probably only looked gentlemanly to those observing. Faith could feel her color rising, and her gaze dropped away from the other men's.

"Let me show you where you will be most comfortable," Renzo said.

"Thank you," Faith murmured. What else could she say? That his fingers were burning into her where they lightly rested on her? That her nerve endings were tingling with awareness? That for the past week she had thought of little else than that kiss they'd shared?

Renzo steered her toward another area of the plane that had a long couch built along one wall and a flat-screen television that rose up from a cabinet at the touch of a button.

"You may watch until we take off," he said. "At that point, it will have to be turned off until we're in the air."

"Thank you," she said stiffly, standing with her hands folded together while she waited for him to return to his engineers. There was a wall between this room and the office he'd been in, and she could no longer see the two men.

Renzo laughed softly. "Relax. No one is going to bite you, *cara*. Unless, of course, you wish it?"

Her heart turned over. His blue gaze glittered hotly, and for one brief moment she thought he might actually pull her into his arms. Shockingly, a part of her wanted him to do so.

But only for a moment, only until she got her senses back and realized what a mistake that would be.

He did not touch her, however, and she began to believe she'd imagined that look that had said he would devour her if she let him. He was toying with her.

"I think I'll be fine without any biting," she said, unable to sound like anything but a prim preacher's daughter as she said it.

He laughed again. "You are a delight, Faith Black." And then he skimmed a finger down her cheek. "But I assure you that you would like it very much if I bit you. I know just where and how to nibble for the most impact."

Faith couldn't breathe. Molten heat rolled through her, pooling between her thighs, making her ache with longing. How did he do it? How did he make her want to forget every last bit of good sense she had and slip between the sheets with him? They were only words, and yet when he spoke them, they were dangerous. Seductive.

"You really shouldn't say things like that," she told him, proud that she managed to speak without choking.

He loomed over her, six feet two inches of gorgeous Italian male who smelled delicious and radiated a lethal sex appeal that had her wanting to wrap herself around him and to hell with the consequences.

Renzo's brow arched mockingly. "And you shouldn't refuse to consider the possibilities."

She had nothing to say to that. Renzo put his hands on her shoulders, then leaned down and brushed his lips across her forehead before turning and leaving without another word.

Her entire body hummed with electricity as she sank onto the couch in a daze. For a whole week, she'd convinced herself that he'd forgotten about their kiss in her apartment, that he'd put it from his mind as inconsequential, that the heat and excitement she'd felt had only been her imagination.

I know just where and how to nibble for the most impact.

Faith shuddered at the images that statement brought to mind. It was a long flight to Rome, and she wasn't going to sleep a wink.

CHAPTER FIVE

THEY arrived in Rome early the next morning. Though Faith had thought she wouldn't sleep at all, she in fact had, and woke feeling somewhat ready for the day. She'd dressed with care in a dark gray suit and heels, and put her hair into a tight knot. If Renzo was planning to work, she was ready.

Her heart had sped up at the sight of him. He'd been sitting in a plush leather chair by a window and sipping a cappuccino while reading something on his mobile tablet. Totally engrossed, he hadn't noticed her at first, and she'd let her eyes feast on him. His dark hair was full and lush, and it still looked slightly wild, as if he'd been racing on the track with the wind blowing through it. Artfully tousled, sexy, as if some woman had been running her fingers through it while he made love to her.

He was dressed in a navy pinstripe suit with a light blue shirt and a dark red tie. On his feet were custom-made Italian loafers. He looked every inch the billionaire and nothing like the daredevil Grand Prix racer at the moment.

She must have made a noise, because he'd lifted his head and spied her there. The frown on his face had not made her happy. No, it had made her feel about two inches tall, but she'd pushed through it and pretended she hadn't noticed while she took her seat in front of him and prepared to go over his appointments.

Now they were in a Mercedes limousine, moving toward the center of Rome, and Faith couldn't help but gape at the sights. She'd never seen anything so old and magnificent in her life. Everywhere you looked, there were crumbling ruins set beside ornate churches, and people moving around as if it were completely ordinary to be surrounded by such beauty.

The early-morning sun shone down on the city, picking out the bright whites of marble monuments and highlighting the red sandstone of ancient ruins. The traffic was heavy as they rounded the Colosseum, and tears pricked at the back of her eyes.

She'd always wanted to see it, and now it was here, huge, sandy-white and red, and imposing against the bright blue Roman sky. There was a cross set in the outer ring of stone that caught her eye.

Renzo looked up then and saw the question in her gaze. "It is actually a church now," he said. "The Pope holds a service in the Colosseum once a year."

Tourists ringed the grounds as they drove around the structure. Soon, they were passing the ruins of the Forum Romanum. People walked along the sidewalks between the Forum and the Colosseum, and vendors lined the way, selling food, scarves and other trinkets. The ride grew bumpy as they drove over the vast swath of cobblestones near the Vittorio Emanuele military monument. Cars converged in the giant circle and honked, scooters blaring past, before traffic straightened out again and they were moving down a narrow street lined with stores and restaurants.

A short while later, the limousine came to a stop on the Via dei Condotti and Renzo's driver hopped out to open the door. Renzo stepped onto the pavement and Faith followed, coming up short when all she saw were high-end fashion stores. Renzo's security emerged from another car, and then Renzo was propelling her toward the nearest shop.

"What are we doing?" she asked as the door swung open to let them into a salon. An expensively dressed woman behind the counter looked up and greeted them in Italian.

Renzo said something to her, and then her eyes slid toward Faith. To the woman's credit, her expression did not change.

"What is going on?" Faith demanded as the woman picked up a phone and made a call.

"You are getting your hair done," Renzo said.

Faith's hand came up to pat her bun. "My hair is fine," she hissed under her breath.

Renzo looked unconvinced. "And I say it is not, *cara*. We are in Italia now, and you are the personal assistant to a very rich man. I cannot have you managing my appointments and greeting my business associates like this."

Faith spluttered. "I look professional. There's nothing wrong with what I'm wearing. Or how I've styled my hair. Your business associates won't care. You are making that up."

"They *will* care. Even my grandmother had more style than you, *piccolo*." He took her briefcase from her numb fingers while her heart throbbed with hurt. "Consider this a part of your salary for accompanying me."

"I like my hair the way it is," she insisted.

He quirked an eyebrow. "Do you realize that in all the time you have worked for me, I've never seen your hair down?"

"I wanted to look professional."

"And you still shall. But with style, *cara mia*."

"I'm not happy with you," Faith said, seething inside and more than a little curious, as well. What would it be like to have a style she could actually manage? Something that gave her more versatility than she had now? She'd always been afraid to let a stylist touch her hair because she didn't know how to communicate what she wanted. What if they cut too much off, or gave her a look she hated?

It wasn't like she could afford the expensive places on Park Avenue where the rich went. No, she was more likely to use the local chop shop equivalent—and did when she got her annual trim. In fairness to Renzo, she had to admit that she made enough money to spring for a nicer salon than a discount place—but she never knew how to find someone she trusted, and therefore she never took the plunge.

Not to mention she saved every dime she could for the down payment on her future home.

Now, however, he was presenting her with the opportunity to use the kind of salon she could never have afforded on her own. The kind of salon the elite frequented.

Renzo gave her that smile that had the power to tilt her world sideways. "You will be happy with me when you are finished. Trust me."

"Fine," she said, arms crossed defensively. "But if I hate it, you're never going to hear the end of it."

Renzo laughed before nodding at the woman who then escorted Faith into the salon and handed her over to a smiling stylist named Giovanna. Thankfully, Giovanna spoke English and put Faith at ease. Before Giovanna made the first cut, Faith discussed her wishes that she be able to keep her hair long. Giovanna listened intently, and then told Faith exactly what she proposed to do.

She didn't cut much length, but she added plenty of layers to make Faith's hair more manageable. An hour later, Faith was staring in the mirror at a woman who had the sleekest, most gorgeously touchable hair imaginable.

"It's amazing," Faith said.

"You have great hair, *signorina*. You only needed a little cut, a little product to make it so." Giovanna spun the chair away from the mirror. "And now a little bit of makeup, *si*? I will teach you how to do a smoky eye, and you will be ready in moments. It is all you will need to drive the men wild."

Ten minutes later, Faith was walking out of the salon and into the reception area where Renzo sat making notes on his tablet. When he looked up and saw her, a little thrill of pleasure shot through her at the shock on his face. He quickly masked it, however, and stood to greet her as if salon appointments were an ordinary part of his day.

"*Fabuloso,* Faith. You look lovely."

Faith was feeling far too happy over her hair to harbor any resentment that he'd basically hauled her into a salon and told her to cut her hair. No, in fact, she was feeling grateful. For the first time, her hair was elegant and chic— but it still felt like her, not like someone else's idea of her.

Her happy feelings began to ebb, however, when Renzo dragged her into a clothing store and arranged an impromptu fashion show in which she was to be the leading lady.

"No," she said as a saleswoman stood patiently by and a group of others hauled clothing into a dressing area. "This is too much, Renzo. I can't accept clothes from you."

His expression was implacable. "Consider it a perk of the job, Faith. I require you to be stylish when you are at my side."

"You never cared before."

He didn't look in the least bit apologetic. "We were in the States. Things were different there. Here, you will be traveling at my side quite frequently and I require you to look the part."

"Look the part of what?" she demanded. "Your latest mistress?"

His gaze grew heated. "Would that be so bad?" he murmured so that no one else could hear.

"Yes," she said automatically, though a part of her was saying no. *Please, yes, now.*

No.

"You will do this, Faith, or you will be on the next flight back to the United States. But think carefully on your answer," he said silkily. "Because, should you choose to go, you will also be without a job."

Fury rolled through her, followed by frustration and a sense that she was in over her head. "That's blackmail."

She wasn't going to give up her job over a wardrobe, and he knew it. That would be a stupid move, no matter how she might wish to see the look of surprise on his face when she said no. A fresh tide of anger rose within her that he would force her into obeying his will.

She had a moment's ugly thought of her father standing over her and telling her she would continue to go to school as before, no matter what people said or did to her, but no matter how angry it made her, she knew this wasn't the same thing. Her father hadn't cared that she would be emotionally scarred by the experience; Renzo was being stubborn over clothing. Not the same at all.

But Renzo was unrepentant. "It is indeed. Now, choose."

Faith's heart throbbed, and her ears were hot with embarrassment. She'd never been the sort of person to draw attention to herself with clothing, but were her clothes really that bad? The gray suit she wore was perfectly serviceable. The skirt hit right below her knees, the jacket hung to midhip, and her shirt was a daring pink. Her heels were black, low and comfortable.

"This isn't necessary," she said. "We could just go to a

department store and spend a lot less money. I only need a few things off-the-rack—"

"Not a chance, *cara*. You represent me, and you will represent me the way I wish you to."

In the end, there was no choice. Faith succumbed to the will of Renzo and the overwhelming force of the saleswomen, who dressed her in outfit after outfit until she actually started to look forward to the next combination they would present her. She'd always worn her suits because she felt comfortable and professional in them. They were off-the-rack, and they fit just fine, but she was redefining what the meaning of a good fit meant as she tried on clothes that seemed tailor-made for her.

The skirts were shorter, but not too much so—right above the knee instead of below it, and fitted to the curve of her hips rather than hanging straight down. The jackets were nipped in at the waist, rounded on the bottom, and cut to right below the waistband of the skirts. There were silky undergarments, belts, trousers, sweaters, dresses, shoes, handbags, scarves and jewelry that went with each outfit. The fabrics were natural, luxurious, rich.

Renzo bore it all with his usual cool efficiency, looking up from his tablet when she emerged each time. He didn't say a word unless there was a disagreement, and he didn't try to force her to choose anything she didn't like. He gave his opinion when asked, and didn't contradict her when she expressed a preference or a dislike of anything in particular.

It wasn't much, but the fact he left her alone to make her choices made her feel somewhat better. It was as if he was telling her that he believed in her judgment, and she appreciated that more than she could say.

After what seemed like hours, the parade came to an end. Renzo said something in Italian, all the saleswomen melted away except for one, and Faith was left standing in the final outfit, a soft, pale green silk dress, belted at the waist, and a pair of sky-high designer heels in a rich cream color. She had to admit she loved the outfit, and hoped it was one they could buy. She felt sophisticated and pretty, like a princess instead of a secretary.

"We are finished here," Renzo said, and she blinked at him.

"But I need to change back into my clothes—"

"Those are your clothes," he told her. "The rest will be sent along."

"The rest?"

"Everything you chose."

"*Everything*?" If she'd had any idea, she would have been more careful. She'd liked so many things. So many *expensive* things. She shook her head. "It's too much. I can never repay you."

Renzo came over and put his hands on her shoulders. In the heels, she didn't have to tilt her head back to look at his expression. His gaze slid down her body, to the buttons on her dress that came together just over her cleavage, and then met her eyes once more while her insides began to melt. "*Mia bella,* it gives me pleasure to do this for you. I have told you before to consider this as a part of your compensation for accompanying me. It is not easy to leave behind one's friends and home, now is it?"

It was when you didn't really have any friends, and the home didn't belong to you, but Faith didn't say that. "I feel like it's too much," she said.

"And I feel like it's not enough. Which of us is right?"

"I'm pretty sure I am. My sense of what things cost is probably more realistic than yours."

Renzo laughed even as he looped her arm in his. "You

are a refreshing woman, Faith. You speak your mind without care for what I might think. I like it."

"You have enough women feeding your ego," she grumbled, and he laughed again.

They exited the shop and got into the waiting car. Faith turned her head to look out the window at the shops opposite, suddenly uncomfortable to be alone with him again. She didn't know why she should be, but she was.

Not because she was afraid of him, but because she was afraid of herself, she realized. The entire time she'd been trying on clothes, she'd been thinking of how he would look at her when she walked out in each outfit. What would Renzo think? What would he do? Would he look at her like he wanted to take her in his arms and kiss her again, the way he had in her apartment?

It was dangerous to think of him like that. Dangerous to think for even a moment that she wanted him to kiss her. There was nothing but heartbreak in allowing herself to think of a man like Renzo wanting her. She was his PA, not his girlfriend.

"I do understand the value of money, *cara*," he said, his voice breaking the silence between them as the car rolled through the streets of Rome. "I was not born rich."

She turned to look at him. She knew that, of course, because she'd read all about him when she'd joined the company. He'd started competing in motorcycle races at seventeen, had been picked up by a major manufacturer and ridden their motorcycles for a few years before coming up with his own designs. He'd poured every euro he had into building his first motorcycle, gotten sponsorship and investors and built D'Angeli Motors into a powerhouse in the industry while others had looked on in shock.

Renzo was formidable, both in his industry and in life, she thought. No wonder he'd maneuvered her so smoothly into changing her hair and buying clothes today. He did not accept defeat. Ever. "Did you grow up in Rome?" she asked.

His gaze was blank. "No. A small town on the Amalfi Coast. My mother was a waitress in a hotel there."

"And your father?"

The corners of his mouth tightened, and a throb of premonition squeezed her heart. "I do not have a father, *cara*."

She didn't quite know what to say to that. She felt like she'd tripped into a minefield, and there was nothing to do now but finish the journey and hope for the best. "I'm sorry, Renzo."

He shrugged. "It has been this way my whole life. I am not bothered by it."

But he was. She could tell by the bleak look on his face, the way his voice was carefully controlled. Whatever it was, it bothered him a great deal.

"My father is a preacher," she said, and then wondered why she'd admitted that to him. But he'd seemed so lost, and she'd found herself wanting to confess that while she had a father, their relationship wasn't perfect.

He looked at her with interest. "A preacher? What is this?"

Faith twisted her fingers together. She didn't like talking about her family. It inevitably brought up painful memories, but she'd started the conversation and had to finish it. "He's a minister. In a church."

"Ah, I see." His gaze was suddenly keen. "Perhaps this explains much about you."

It explained a lot, actually, but she was far too embarrassed to tell him all of it. "He was a hard man to live with," she said softly. "He expected much out of his children. I was the disappointment. My brother Albert was an Eagle Scout, and I…"

She swallowed. Renzo reached for her hand. She let him take it, a little tingle of awareness beginning to sizzle up her spine as he threaded his fingers in hers.

"All children think they are a disappointment at one time or another. It is rarely true, I believe."

"It is definitely true in my case," Faith said. "I haven't spoken to my father in eight years."

His eyes searched hers, their blue depths full of dark emotion. "I'm sorry, Faith. I can tell this upsets you."

She shrugged. But yes, it hurt, even after all this time. She'd been so stupid. So naive and innocent and gullible. And she'd paid the price. Jason hadn't. He was a male, and males stuck together.

"I, um, I shouldn't have said anything," she replied, her gaze firmly fixed on their linked hands. "It makes me uncomfortable to talk about it."

He brought her hand to his mouth and feathered his lips across her skin. His breath was hot as he spoke. "Then we will not speak of it again."

Tears pricked her eyes. She really didn't want to like him, and yet she couldn't quite help it at the moment. "Thank you."

"It is nothing," he said. And then his voice grew firm, determined. "You are a good woman, Faith. Never believe otherwise."

"You don't really know me," she said. "I might be nothing more than a very good actress."

At that he laughed. "Actually, you aren't an actress at all," he told her. "Your every emotion is written across your face. Would you like to know what I see there now?"

She met his gaze evenly. His eyes glittered with heat and promise, and she could feel her nipples responding, tightening, her breasts growing heavy and firm. Her sex throbbed with need, her body growing tight and achy.

"What do you see?" she asked, surprised at the husky turn of her voice.

He lifted his hand to her face, traced his thumb across her bottom lip. She bit back the moan that wanted to escape as he did so. "I see a woman who wants me…but who is terribly afraid to admit it."

CHAPTER SIX

"You are mistaken, Renzo," Faith said once she found her voice again. Her heart, in the meantime, was pounding at light speed. "You really should see a doctor about that ego, you know. It must be such a burden carrying that thing around."

One corner of his mouth lifted in a grin. "You amuse me, and yet I recognize this tactic. It's not working, by the way."

"Tactic? What tactic? I assure you I'm only speaking the truth."

He leaned toward her, his eyes gleaming hotly. "Then prove it to me, *cara mia*. Kiss me and prove to me that you are unaffected."

Faith sat stiffly beside him, lacing her fingers together in her lap. "That would be unprofessional, Mr. D'Angeli."

He lounged back on the seat, watching her with dark humor sparking in his gaze. "Another tactic, lovely Faith. First you insult me. Then you wish to distance me with your formality."

"I'm your PA," she said. "It's perfectly appropriate."

"But aren't you curious?"

Her heart thumped at the wicked sparkle in his gaze. Of course she was curious. "Not at all." She smoothed the fabric of the green dress. "Honestly, does this usually work for you? I'd have thought you had much more complex methods to employ."

He laughed. And then he leaned toward her and it was everything she could do not to scoot away and cling to the door like a frightened virgin. "You try to push me away with your thorniness, but it doesn't work the way you suppose it does, *cara mia*."

She drew her body upright, holding herself rigid in the seat. "Then you are not as smart as I thought you were. A shame, considering how many people depend upon you."

His eyes narrowed. "Do you know what you need, Faith?"

"Sleep," she ventured. "I didn't get a lot of it last night."

One eyebrow lifted. "What I propose does involve a bed, but sleep isn't part of the equation. At least not immediately."

She turned her head away to hide the blush that she knew was creeping up her neck and spreading over her cheeks. A moment later Renzo gasped. She turned, her heart tumbling at the anguish tightening his features. He clenched his fists at his sides, and his lips were white with pain.

"Renzo, are you all right? Is it your leg?"

He nodded once, and she sidled toward him, suddenly uncaring about keeping her distance. "Stretch your leg out if you can. Let me massage it."

His head fell back against the seat, his skin turning ashen as he stretched the leg. She had no doubt he was in agony. "*Dio*, it hurts," he said.

"Do you have any pain pills?"

"I do, but I took one last night. I can't take another for a few days yet."

His muscles were so tight. Faith massaged rhythmically, trying to ease the cramp. "Why not?"

His blue gaze pierced into her, the depths filled with pain and even perhaps a little bit of fear. "They are addictive, Faith. I can't allow that to happen."

No, a man like Renzo would not wish to be addicted to painkillers. She admired his willpower even though she feared he might be a bit too strict with parceling out the pills. "What about anti-inflammatories? Surely you can take those."

"*Si.*"

Faith grabbed her purse and dug through it until she found a bottle. "Here, I have something. They're over the counter and completely safe."

He blinked at her. "And why do you need these?" he asked, accepting the two pills she shook into his palm.

"My wrists sometimes hurt at the end of a long work day. Typing," she added when he continued to look perplexed. She poured water into one of the crystal goblets set against one wall of the limousine and handed it to him. He put the pills in his mouth and drank, and Faith continued to massage his leg until he grasped her hands and pulled her against him, wedging her into the curve of his body where he lay back against the seat.

"Just sit with me," he said softly, his breath ruffling her hair. "That is all I want."

"But your leg—"

"The spasm is easing. It does not always last long. Thankfully, this is one of those times."

Faith thought she should move away from him, but she couldn't do it. She could feel the tension in his body and knew he still hurt, so she leaned against him and sat very still. The heat of his body slid beneath her skin, the sensation both thrilling and comforting. His hand came up to stroke her hair, and goose bumps prickled along the back of her neck.

This was wrong, so wrong. And yet it felt too good.

They didn't speak, and eventually her eyes started to feel heavy, her body languid. Soon, in spite of her attempts otherwise, she fell asleep against Renzo. When she awoke, the car had stopped and Renzo was gently shaking her.

Faith pushed upright, horrified with herself for falling asleep on him. "I'm sorry."

Renzo was smiling. "For what? Being tired? I rather enjoyed it, *cara*. You are incapable of being prickly when you are asleep."

Faith smoothed her hair, certain it must be a wild mess, and dug through her purse for her mirror, praying to God she hadn't drooled in her sleep. Or that she wasn't now sporting raccoon eyes. A quick check in her compact assured her that she still looked presentable, once she slid her fingers through her hair to tame any flyaways.

Renzo exited the vehicle and stood waiting for her while a bevy of uniformed staff swarmed around the car, sorting luggage and packages and carting them into the house. Faith blinked at the facade in front of her. The stone house had that timeworn ocher color that only seemed to exist in Italy. It was less ornate than she'd expected it would be, and she stood with her head tilted back, taking in the wooden shutters and twining bougainvillea and climbing roses that graced both corners of the home. Spilling from each window was a profusion of bright red blooms.

"Do you like it?" Renzo asked.

"It's lovely."

"Then look this way," he said, turning her until she was facing a long slope of garden that butted up against a stone wall—beyond which was a beautiful valley dotted with tall cypresses, yellow fields, purple flowers, green grass and lush vineyards as far as the eye could see.

"We aren't in Rome?" she asked dumbly. How long had she slept anyway?

Renzo laughed. "No. This is my home in Tuscany. We are closer to Florence than Rome now."

"I…I missed it all," she said. Disappointment ate at her.

"You were tired, *cara*. Besides, there will be plenty of opportunities to see the countryside again." He tucked her arm in his and led her toward the house. "Now, however, you will wish to rest and freshen up. There is a party tonight."

Her heart fell. "Tonight?"

"You are nervous?" he asked gently, stopping to face her.

Yes, but she wouldn't admit that. Faith swallowed. What if there were photographers? What if someone back in Cottonwood saw her in a tabloid? Would they recognize her? She thought of her past coming back to haunt her now, after she'd run so far and done so much to change who she was, and felt sick.

"I—I was thinking you might want to rest," she said, letting her gaze drop briefly to his leg.

His expression shuttered when she met his eyes again. "I appreciate the concern, *cara*, but it is not necessary. There is much to be done in the next few weeks and little time to waste."

She wanted to tell him that looking after his health wasn't a waste of time, but she knew he didn't want to hear it. Renzo was determined to ride the Viper even if it killed him. She shoved down the feeling of panic that seemed determined to wrap around her throat and faced him squarely. She wasn't sure if the panic came from her fear of discovery or her fear for him—or both, more likely—but she didn't want to think about it any longer.

"Then perhaps we should work on your schedule for a

while," she said briskly, attempting to be all business and hoping he didn't see that she was upset.

He studied her for a moment before his sexy mouth curved into a smile that made her heart skip a beat. "*Si*, this is a very good idea. Next week, I take the Viper onto the track to begin training. I will have little time for business meetings then."

Faith's heart thumped in slow motion. "Next week? Is it ready so soon?"

Excitement danced in his eyes while her stomach twisted in fear. "It is."

And Renzo would be flying around a track at speeds approaching, perhaps exceeding, two hundred miles per hour. With a leg that could cramp at any moment and render him incapable of controlling the motorcycle.

Faith didn't want to think about the consequences of that scenario. Instead, she threw herself into her work once they reached Renzo's home office. They worked for a couple of hours, and then Renzo pushed back from his desk and told her to go get some rest.

"I'm fine," she said.

"Your eyes keep closing. You can hardly keep them open."

It was true, but he'd shown no signs of being tired and so she'd kept on working. "It's called blinking," she said stubbornly.

Renzo laughed. "Indeed." He got to his feet and stretched. "Nevertheless, go to your room and blink there. I am going to do the same. Come, I will show you where you are staying."

Faith followed him up the wide marble staircase that sat imposingly at the center of the house. She could hardly keep from gawking as they'd walked through the villa. It was lovely, with marble floors, Oriental rugs, old oil paintings and tapestries on the walls, and vases of flowers filling every surface. There were antiques mixed with modern furnishings, giving it all an eclectic and lush feeling.

It was as sumptuous as the Stein's penthouse, and yet it was more livable. The kind of place where you could actually put your feet on a table and not be too worried that you were mistaking some sort of modern art piece for a footstool.

Renzo led her down a long hallway with tall doors that opened to bedrooms filled with light. The last one was hers, he told her, and she stepped into the room, certain he'd made a mistake. This was the kind of room you gave to guests, not employees. There was a huge tester bed covered in white linen, antique wardrobes for her clothing, a delicate writing desk by a window, and silk chairs and a couch where she could lounge in the evenings. There was even a television, and three sets of tall windows, which opened onto a balcony with a table and chairs.

Perfect for morning coffee, she thought.

"Do you approve?" he asked as she stood with her back to him and gaped. It was like something out of a travel fairy tale—the kind of thing you dreamed of when you read about Tuscany and imagined yourself living there.

Faith turned to him. "It's lovely, Renzo. Thank you."

"I am glad you are pleased." He came over and put his hands on her shoulders, skimmed them down her arms. "I am across the hall, *cara*, should you require anything."

Faith bit the inside of her lip. "I—I'm sure I'll be fine. But thank you."

His smile was wickedly sensual. "Nevertheless," he said as he bent and kissed her on both cheeks while a tidal wave of flame rolled through her, "I am there."

The party, it turned out, was being held in a villa nearby. Faith slept for a couple of hours, and then dressed in a figure-skimming red cocktail dress with a halter top that kept her modest and a pair of silver strappy heels that made her feel like a princess. She'd asked Renzo why she needed to go along earlier when they were working, and he'd looked at her with that gorgeous broody look he got and told her she was going because he'd realized after the Stein's party that she was good repellant.

"Repellant?" she'd asked, certain her puzzled frown must have amused him.

"Female repellant," he'd deadpanned before going on to explain that he did not need the distractions of women in his life right now.

"And what am I?" Faith murmured as she studied herself in the mirror. Especially when she considered the way he'd told her that he was across the hall if she needed anything.

Anything, he'd stressed. Faith shivered as she remembered the feel of his lips on her cheeks, the imprint of his fingers on her arms.

Renzo D'Angeli was a very confusing man, she decided. And very sexy, a little voice added.

Faith ran the brush through her hair one last time. She didn't look half-bad, though she still wasn't in the same league as the Katie Palmers of the world. Her hair was smooth and golden, hanging down her back in a lustrous fall, and her eyes really stood out with the addition of eye shadow, liner and mascara.

It was her in the mirror, and not her. Her as she'd never been, she amended. She hadn't been allowed to wear makeup when she was growing up, and she'd never been allowed to do anything with her hair other than leave it long. As the daughter of a preacher, she'd been required to be as plain and circumspect as possible.

Until the day she hadn't been.

Faith turned away from the mirror and grabbed her

wrap and tiny purse. Then she hurried downstairs to meet Renzo. As she reached the bottom of the stairs, the butler came forward to greet her in impeccable English.

"*Signorina,*" he began, "Signore D'Angeli had business to attend to in town. He asked me to let you know that he would meet you at the party."

"*Grazie,*" Faith replied, her heart sinking.

She wasn't thrilled with the idea of going alone, but she went outside to get into the waiting car. The ride didn't last long, but since it was dark she didn't see anything along the way, until they arrived at a grand villa with lights spilling out of the windows and people mingling on the grounds and inside the house.

Faith exited the car and stood with her purse clutched to her body like a shield while the chauffeur drove away. Her pulse was tripping along recklessly and she took deep breaths, telling herself not to freak out. There was no sign of a photographer anyhow, was there? Perhaps arriving alone was a good thing, since Renzo was the main attraction for paparazzi. If she just stayed in the background, she would be fine.

"*Buona notte,*" a voice said before a man strolled toward her from the garden.

"H-hello," she said as he stepped into the light. If Renzo was the most handsome man on the planet, then this man was surely second. He was tall, broad and lean—and she knew who he was. She'd seen his picture in the same motorcycle magazines in which she'd seen Renzo's.

"Ah, English," he said. "You are American, no?"

Faith swallowed. "Yes."

The man held out his hand. "Niccolo Gavretti. But you can call me Nico."

"I know who you are," Faith said as she accepted his handshake. "I'm Faith Black."

Nico's handsome face split in a grin. "Ah, Faith, I have heard of you. Renzo's prized secretary, yes?" His dark gaze slid down her body. "I see why he keeps you hidden away in America. *Bella.*"

Faith extracted her hand when he tried to hold it for longer than necessary. "No one keeps me hidden. I've only worked for Mr. D'Angeli for six months."

Nico didn't stop smiling. "Better and better," he said. "And yet I am glad you are here now."

"I don't see why you should be," she said. He was incredibly handsome, but he didn't make her heart throb the way Renzo did. He was, like Renzo, a player of the worst sort. Women flowed in and out of his bed like water from a faucet.

He laughed. "You are a beautiful woman. Why should I not be? Unless, of course, you are spoken for already?"

Faith felt herself reddening, though she knew he was only flattering her because it was as second nature to him as breathing. "If you will excuse me, I need to find my boss."

"I will take you to him," Nico said, offering his arm. "You will never find him in this crush without help."

Faith hesitated. It was true the place was overrun with elegantly dressed people. And she spoke no Italian. She'd found a man who spoke English, and who knew Renzo. But she seemed to remember reading that Nico and Renzo were rivals on the track. And she knew for a fact that Renzo was determined to bring out his latest production bike before Gavretti Manufacturing could unveil theirs.

"Afraid of what Renzo will say?" Nico asked.

Faith lifted her chin. "No, of course not."

"Then come with me, *bella*, and we will find him."

Renzo arrived at the party later than he'd thought he would. But he'd gotten a call from one of his investors and he'd needed to go into Florence for a meeting. He'd fully intended to be back by the time Faith left, but he was nearly an hour late. She would, no doubt, be furious with him. He'd sent her into this gathering alone when he should have gone back for her and to hell with the time.

Now, he stood at the edge of the glittering crowd congregating in the garden and scanned it for a sighting of her. He knew she was here because Ennio had still been out front with the car when he'd arrived. Since Renzo had driven his own car, he'd sent Ennio home and then come to look for Faith. He'd tried calling her mobile phone, but she was not answering.

The hostess smiled when she saw him. "Renzo, darling, we're so glad you've returned to Italia," Filomena Mazzaro said. "How is the new motorbike coming along?"

Renzo didn't feel like talking to anyone until he found Faith, but he chatted for a moment before asking if Filomena had seen her. Filomena's brows drew together. "I don't remember greeting her, no. But I am sure she is here, darling. We have so many people tonight."

Renzo excused himself after a few more moments and continued the search. He should have asked Faith what she was planning to wear tonight, but how well would that have worked? She was a woman, and no doubt had changed her dress at least three times before deciding.

He drew up short when he spotted Niccolo Gavretti. He'd known Gavretti would be here, but he didn't particularly feel like dealing with the man tonight.

Perhaps he wouldn't have to. Gavretti was standing with a blonde in a red dress, and he seemed engrossed in her. He had his hand on her shoulder as he smiled down at her. He looked as if he wanted to kiss her, but she took a step to the side the moment his head dipped. Renzo laughed to himself. He couldn't see the blonde's face because the instant she'd stepped aside, a light had shone straight into his eyes, silhouetting her form.

She was, of course, voluptuous. He could tell that much. She had full, lush breasts and a nipped-in waist that flared out again in generous hips. Her legs were long and lovely, her feet encased in delicate shoes with glittery silver straps. Everything a woman ought to be, he decided. Gavretti had excellent taste, as he well knew from the days when they used to prowl the bars of Florence together, drinking and having a good time.

The blonde might be gorgeous, but Renzo wasn't interested in her. He had to find Faith. He started to walk past the two of them, but the woman cried out as he did so.

The voice was painfully familiar. Renzo stiffened as if he'd been struck by lightning. Slowly, he turned. The voluptuous blonde stared back at him, her green eyes wide, her lips red and luscious and kissable.

Kissable. Maldedizone.

Faith sashayed over to him while Gavretti smirked. The bastard.

"I've been looking for you, Faith," Renzo said calmly. He was proud of himself for how calm he sounded. How reasonable.

She was beautiful. Utterly gorgeous, and he was a fool for allowing her to come alone.

"I've been looking for you, too," she said. "Nico was helping me."

Renzo's lips peeled back from his teeth in a smile. He'd seen how Gavretti was helping her. The hard bite of acid flooded his throat as he thought of Gavretti's hand on her— of his attempt to kiss her. Kiss *his* Faith. It wasn't the first time Gavretti had tried to take something from Renzo that did not belong to him. "Was he? How wonderfully chivalrous of him."

Renzo slipped an arm around her lush form, anchored her to him. She gasped, the smallest intake of breath, and his body responded, tightening, hardening. He wanted her beneath him, making those noises while he took her to heaven and back. While he got her out of his system so he could concentrate again.

Because he'd been thinking of little else but getting her naked since this afternoon, when she'd transformed before his eyes. He should have known better. He'd already been attracted to her, inexplicably perhaps, but now? Now he wanted to mark her as his and kill any man who dared to touch her.

Gavretti's eyes narrowed as his gaze slipped back and forth between them. "If I had known she was yours, Renzo—"

"She is," he stated with finality.

He could feel Faith stiffening in outrage. Because she did not yet realize the truth. "Renzo, I am not—"

He cupped her jaw and slanted his mouth over hers, silencing her.

CHAPTER SEVEN

FAITH was furious. She sat in Renzo's sports car, her arms folded over her breasts and her head turned toward the window, seething. Renzo shifted smoothly, the engine revving into the night as the car raced along the Tuscan roads toward his villa.

How dared he? First, Niccolo Gavretti had thought he could have his way with her, and then Renzo had come along—hot, furious and broody as hell—and the standoff had begun. It wasn't about her—it was about who was in control, about who got what he wanted.

Renzo had kissed her in front of all those people while cameras flashed and caught the moment forever. Her heart did a long slide into the bottom of her stomach. It had only been a matter of time before she was photographed with Renzo, so she could hardly be surprised about it.

And yet the panic that clawed into her now wouldn't go away. She'd done nothing wrong. Not now, and not eight years ago. But she dreaded the attention if that old photograph was brought to light. The shame and helpless rage.

What angered her most about tonight was that Renzo hadn't kissed her because he'd wanted to, but because he'd wanted to prove something to Nico. He'd been marking her as his, but only because he knew it would irritate the other man.

The moment he'd let her go, she'd turned on her heel and marched for the door. It was the calmest, most rational response she'd been capable of, since staying there would have necessitated her slapping the both of them.

Renzo hadn't argued when she'd told him she wanted to go. He'd simply led the way to his car and roared out of the driveway without saying another word.

Now, the car ate up the roadway until Faith's heart began to beat hard for a different reason. "Renzo, you're scaring me. This isn't the track."

He swore, but the car throttled back to a more-reasonable speed. His hands flexed on the wheel, and his handsome face was harsh in the lights from the dash. He looked furious, which only fueled her anger.

"I don't know why you're angry," she said. "I'm not the one who embarrassed you by kissing you in front of all those people."

He shot her a disbelieving glance. "You're embarrassed? Over what?"

She turned toward him, arms still crossed, her heart racing. It was merely a game to him, while to her it could mean being the subject of public scrutiny again. "I realize that you may think you're God's gift—heaven knows enough women have told you so—but not everyone wants their private life put on display for the world to see. Not only that, but we *have* no private life! You did it just to prove a point to Nico."

His eyes flashed. "Do not call that man Nico," he growled. "He only wanted to use you so he could get to me."

Another spike of anger launched her blood pressure into the danger zone. "Do you think I don't know that? I'm not stupid, Renzo. Two of Italy's most famous bachelors fighting over me? I hardly think so. I just happened to be the bone that both dogs decided they wanted to control tonight. If there had been a juicy steak nearby, they'd have fought over that instead."

Renzo swore again. And then he jerked the car off the road and onto a narrow dirt track she hadn't seen before he turned. The car jolted to a stop and then he unsnapped her seat belt and reached for her before she knew what he was planning.

He crushed her mouth beneath his, his fingers sliding into her hair, his tongue demanding entrance. She opened to him, too shocked by the onslaught to protest. She should be angry. She should push him away. She should do anything but let him kiss her as if he were a dying man and she the last hope he had for salvation.

But, shockingly, she was turned on. Her body was on fire. Her nerve endings were zinging with sparks and her sex ached for his possession. She was throbbing, aching, melting—needing things she'd never needed before.

His tongue delved deep, demanding that she meet him, that she give him everything.

She did.

He slid one hand up her thigh, beneath the hem of her dress. Part of her wanted to clamp her legs together, to tell him no, but that was her father talking. Her damned childhood talking.

She was a woman, and she was capable of wanting a man, of choosing the man who would be her first. It wasn't wrong or ugly to feel this way. It was a revelation.

A glorious, exciting, shattering revelation.

Renzo's fingers spread along her hip, shaped her as she tried to get closer to him. When his hand slid over her panties, she had to force herself to keep breathing. She did not know what he would do, but she found herself hoping he would touch her. Dying for him to touch her.

And frightened, too.

And then he slid one finger across the thin silk, and then down…down over the damp heat of her. The groan that emanated from his throat vibrated into her. Thrilled her.

His finger stroked over her again, eliciting a moan. Every thought in her head flew out the window. All she wanted was to feel more of this delicious sensation, this wicked pleasure. He kissed her hard, and she shuddered and arched against his hand, wanting the barrier gone, wanting to feel everything.

She wanted more. *More*.

He skimmed his mouth down her throat, leaving a trail of hot kisses as the temperature in the car spiked. Faith closed her eyes, gasping at the sensual onslaught.

"I want you, Faith. I *want* you. It has nothing to do with Gavretti, nothing to do with anyone but you. I want to take you to my bed and spend the night lost in your body. I've been imagining all the things I want to do to you for the past week. All the ways in which I want to explore you."

His voice was deep, his Italian accent thicker than usual, and his words so sexy she could die. His words shocked her. Turned her on. She wanted to know what sort of things he'd imagined. Wanted to know what he would do if she said yes.

But she was cautious. Scared. She wasn't sophisticated enough to know how this worked or what tomorrow would bring if she said the yes he wanted her to say. The yes she was dying to say.

"I—I'm not sure this is a good idea," she said quickly. "This isn't part of my job—"

He pulled away from her suddenly. And then he swore in Italian, the words hot and sharp and nothing like the sexy words he'd just said to her. Faith wanted to cry at the loss of his heat.

He pounded the steering wheel once, a sharp, violent move that made her jump. And then he shoved a hand through his hair before turning the key. The car roared to life again, the dash lights illuminating the harsh lines of his jaw. Disappointment rolled through her, along with a healthy dose of regret. Why had she spoken? Why had she pierced the happiness that had been racing through her body like a nuclear explosion?

He turned to look at her, his blue eyes penetrating even in the darkness. "I would never pay a woman—*any* woman—to have sex with me, Faith. Do you understand that?"

"I wasn't suggesting—"

"You were," he snapped. "You keep throwing your job at me, as if I have no idea what it is I pay you for."

Her heart throbbed because she knew he was right.

He reversed onto the roadway and popped the car into gear before turning to her again. "I assure you that I know exactly what I pay you for. And I want you because you are beautiful and fascinating, not because you're convenient. If you believe that, then by all means go to bed alone tonight."

Faith couldn't sleep. Partly, it was the jetlag. And, partly, it was the adrenaline still coursing through her body after the way Renzo had kissed her in his car. She'd been so close to heaven, and so far at the same time.

It shocked her to admit it, but she'd wanted him with a fierceness that she would never have believed possible only a week ago. That was the power of Renzo D'Angeli, she thought sourly. He was gorgeous, compelling and utterly amazing. When he turned all that male power on you, you wanted to let him continue until the very end. Until you were a sobbing mess begging him for another chance.

What else explained the way women kept throwing

themselves at him, despite his reputation for never staying with one woman longer than a couple of months?

Nothing. And she was little different, apparently. Renzo was a flame that she wanted to immolate herself in—even though she knew she shouldn't. Pitiful. For all her professionalism, for all her belief that she alone would be immune to him, she was no different from the rest.

Faith threw the covers back and yanked on her robe. She owed him an explanation for the way she'd behaved, but it would have to wait until morning. She'd insulted him, and she hadn't meant to do so. But she'd been confused, scared, and she'd said the first thing that had popped into her head.

The wrong thing.

From the beginning, Renzo had made it clear that the decisions about what she did were hers to make. The decision to go to the party at the Stein's, though he'd cajoled pretty hard. The decision to come to Italy. Even the decisions about how to style her hair and what to wear, though he'd forced her into making the choices in the first place. He had not once told her how things would be, though he'd certainly pushed her into action.

Renzo might be her employer, but he would not ever expect it to give him access to her body. She knew better, and yet she'd implied he'd believed it did.

Faith's stomach growled, and she realized she'd failed to eat at the party. She'd been nervous, waiting for Renzo to arrive, trying to hold her own with Niccolo Gavretti—who had refused to let her search for Renzo by herself. Well, now she knew why. No doubt he'd orchestrated that moment when he'd tried to kiss her precisely because he knew Renzo was watching.

Clearly, there was something more between them than simple rivalry—and she'd been the one caught in the middle of their feud tonight, the collateral damage as they waged their war against each other.

Faith slipped from her room, hesitating at Renzo's door when she saw a light coming from underneath it, but continued down the hall and then down the marble staircase to the large kitchen at the back of the house.

She found a loaf of bread on the counter and some cheese in the fridge, and then dug around for a knife with which to slice them. Once she'd fixed a small plate, she turned to go back to her room, but stopped when a shadow moved outside the door. Her heart lodged in her throat and she wondered for a moment if she should scream, but then the door opened and a man stepped inside.

A man with a tiny, mewling bundle in his arms.

"Renzo?"

He looked up as if he'd just realized she was there. The kitten mewed again, such a sad, pitiful little sound, and Faith's heart squeezed tight.

Renzo came toward her and set the kitten on the large island, blocking the tiny thing from escaping. "I kept hearing something outside my window," he said. "I couldn't find the mother, or any trace of other kittens. I think maybe she moved the litter and forgot one."

"It's so little. It can't be more than a month old."

Renzo picked the creature up again and held it out to her. "You know what to do with cats, *si*?"

She took the kitten, a lump forming in her throat as it shivered hard. "He—or she—probably needs milk," Faith said. "But we have to warm it up. Cold milk won't do. It'll make his belly ache."

Renzo moved to the refrigerator and took out the milk. Then he found a saucepan and poured some in before setting it on the stove and turning on the burner. His hair was disheveled, and she realized for the first time that he wasn't wearing a shirt. His broad chest was muscled, firm, and she found her breath shortening as she watched him move.

He wore a pair of sleep pants with a drawstring tie that hung low on his hips, revealing the tight ridges of his abdomen and the arrow of dark hair that disappeared beneath the waist of his pants.

"He must have been terribly loud if you could hear him in your room," she said, hugging the kitten close and stroking the silky fur. She'd missed having a cat since Mr. Darcy had died last year. The little body began to rumble with a purr instead of a shiver, and tears filled Faith's eyes as she thought of the kitten lost and scared.

Renzo turned from the stove and leaned against the counter, crossing one leg over another as he stood there looking at her. "*Si*. I did not realize it was a cat at first, the whine was so high-pitched. He was in the bougainvillea beneath my windows. If I had not been standing on the balcony, I would not have heard him."

"He's lucky you went looking for him," she said.

"I could not leave him there."

"No."

After a moment, Renzo turned and rummaged in a cabinet for a small bowl. Then he stuck his finger into the milk on the stove, testing it. Faith's heart did a little skip at that sign of tenderness in such a hard man.

"It is ready," he said, pouring the milk and bringing the bowl over to the island. Faith set the kitten down and he immediately began to drink. His purr grew louder, and she glanced at Renzo. They laughed together.

"He is as loud as the Viper," Renzo said. "Perhaps we should call him that."

Faith felt heat curling through her stomach, her limbs. "We don't actually know it's a he," she pointed out. "He might be a she."

"Ah, then we will have to call her Miss Viper."

"You would keep this cat?" she asked.

"No," he said softly. "I would give him—or her—to you. Because you miss having a cat."

Her eyes were stinging. "I don't have time for a pet," she said. "I'm away from home too much, working...." She let her voice trail off as the word brought back memories of earlier.

"I'm sorry," he said, and she looked up again, met his gaze.

"For what?"

He shrugged. "For what happened in the car. I was... angry. I should not have kissed you like that."

"I didn't mind the kiss," she said softly, dropping her gaze again as her blood fizzed in her veins at the memory of all that heat and passion. "Renzo, I..."

She stroked the kitten's soft fur, unsure she could say the words she needed to say.

Renzo reached out and put his hand over hers, oh so lightly, and stroked the kitten with her for a moment. Then his hand dropped away, rested on the counter. "What is it, Faith?"

"I'm sorry, too," she said, forcing herself to meet his gaze. "I shouldn't have mentioned work. I know you wouldn't—" She stopped, swallowed. "I know that you don't expect me to sleep with you simply because I'm your PA."

"No," he said, "I don't. If you sleep with me, Faith, it will be because you want to. Because you cannot imagine another day without giving in to this passion between us."

"I don't know what passion is," she said hurriedly, before she lost her nerve. "I—I've never..." Her voice trailed off as her courage fizzled.

He tilted her chin up until she was looking at him, his

blue gaze searching hers. "You have never what, Faith? Slept with someone you worked with?"

Her laugh was strangled. "No, that's not it. I've never, um…slept…with anyone."

He was utterly silent. The only sound in the room was the kitten purring and lapping milk. Her heart was thrumming hard, and a rush of heat climbed into her cheeks, bloomed between her breasts. She was hot, so hot, and she wanted to take off her robe and slip beneath a cool spray of water.

"You are untouched?"

Untouched. It was such a quaint word, and yet it was less shocking than the other word he could have used. *Virgin.*

Faith nodded.

Renzo slid a hand through his hair and swore softly. "You have stunned me, Faith Black, and I am not easily stunned."

She tried to laugh it off. "I'm a preacher's daughter. What did you expect?"

"Yes, but you've been away from home for, presumably, eight years now. In all this time, you did not find someone you wanted to be with?"

Not until now.

Faith sighed. She was in so much trouble here. And not just because she was alone with a man she desperately wanted. No, it was worse. Much worse. Because she was at least half in love with him already.

He was kinder than she'd expected, more considerate, and he cared about tiny, helpless animals. It was more than she'd thought he was capable of just two weeks ago when she'd watched him leave the office with Katie Palmer on his arm. He'd been so remote then, so perfect and untouchable and polished. Not at all the kind of man who would warm milk for a kitten in the middle of the night.

Faith bit down on the inside of her lip. She wasn't *really* in love with him—but she could be if he kept doing things that made her heart tighten in her chest.

"It's not that simple," she said.

"I don't see why not."

She picked the kitten up again because it had finished drinking and was starting to wander. "Because it's different for a woman."

He reached out, stroked the kitten's head. "Do you know how to tell if it is a boy or a girl?"

Faith carried the kitten over to the window where a shaft of moonlight pooled over the kitchen sink. "Looks like a girl," she said after she held it up to the light, relieved that Renzo had decided to talk about something else.

"Ah, so Miss Viper it is. But that is not so pretty, is it?" he said, frowning.

"It is a bit much for such a little one," Faith replied.

"We could call her *Piccolo*."

"What does that mean?" He'd said that word to her earlier today, and she'd wondered then.

"Little one."

It was certainly appropriate, at least for the kitten. But still not quite right. Faith frowned, thinking. And then it hit her. "I think she is a Lola."

Renzo smiled. "*Si,* Lola is perfect. What do you recommend we do with her now that she has eaten?"

"She'll need a place to sleep," Faith said. "She'll need something to burrow into, and a small space where she can't get into trouble."

"Then we will find something for her."

They hunted through the kitchen until Renzo found an empty wine crate in the pantry. Then he retrieved a blanket from a closet and mounded it in the center. After they found another small box to make into a litter pan, Renzo helped her carry everything up to her room. They put Lola into a small walk-in closet off the bathroom and closed the door.

She mewed for a few moments while they stood there looking at each other in silence, hoping she would settle down. She did, and they crept from the bathroom, closing the door behind them.

Moonlight slanted through the long windows, illuminating Renzo's form as he stood in the center of her room. His skin looked warm, silky, and she realized with a jolt that she ached to touch him. To press her lips to his skin and see if he tasted as delicious as he looked.

"A virgin shouldn't look at a man the way you're looking at me," he said, an edge of strain in his voice.

"I'm sorry," she said automatically, ducking her head in embarrassment.

He closed the distance between them until he was standing so close that his heat enveloped her and her body began to soften and melt. It was novel. Her nipples were tingling, tightening, her sex aching with renewed want. If he spread her robe and slipped her gown off, she would be incapable of protest.

She wanted him to do it, and she feared he would at the same time.

Renzo lifted his fingers to her cheek, skimmed lightly over her flesh. "I'm sorry, too," he said. "It seems as if I am filled with nothing but apologies tonight. But, Faith, I see now that it would be wrong to take you to my bed. If you were experienced…"

Disappointment filled her. And a thread of anger snagged through the disappointment, pulling the fabric of it taut. "I see," she said primly, because she couldn't make herself say anything else. How could she be angry when only a moment before she'd been afraid?

"You are angry," he said. "I understand. But you've

saved yourself for a reason, Faith, and you shouldn't take that next step lightly."

She hadn't exactly saved herself so much as she'd had no opportunities. She hadn't dated very much, because she didn't trust men after Jason—and when she had dated, she'd inevitably broken the relationship off before they ever reached a point at which she might consider having sex. How did she know, if she got that far, that a man wouldn't violate her trust again?

Maybe it was a good thing this was happening. Because she wouldn't have to deal with the inevitable embarrassment and broken heart when Renzo grew tired of her.

"You're wrong," she said coolly, because she refused to let him see that he'd hurt her. "I'm not angry. I'm just tired. I think you've misread the situation entirely. I was not inviting you into my bed at all."

His hand dropped away. Somehow, she managed not to whimper. Not to beg him to touch her again.

"Then I will leave you to your rest," he said, his voice so cool it chilled her. Then he strode past her without another word and walked out the door.

After he was gone, Faith threw herself onto the bed in a dramatic maneuver worthy of generations of Southern women, and cried into her pillow. Angry tears, she told herself. Angry, frustrated, bitter tears.

CHAPTER EIGHT

RENZO could hardly wrap his head around the fact that his sexy PA was still a virgin. How was this possible when she was so passionate beneath the prim exterior? This was a woman who kissed with her whole body. She focused every bit of concentration she had on the meeting of lips and tongues, and the effect was exquisite.

Renzo shifted at his desk as his body began to react to the memory of kissing her last night in his car. She'd been like a living flame in his arms, and he'd wanted to burn himself up in her. When he'd encountered the damp evidence of her desire for him, it had been all he could do not to rip the thin silk from her body and bury himself inside her then and there.

Thankfully he had not, since she was a virgin. Not only would she likely not have appreciated such an introduction to lovemaking, but what if she took it too seriously? What if she thought that because they'd had sex, they had a future together?

Faith was serious, proper, a preacher's daughter. She'd probably want to get married, have babies, do charity work, hostess parties and drag him to school functions.

He did not know that for a fact, but if it was true, he did not want to hurt her when she learned he wanted none of those things. He wasn't against marriage or babies in principle, but he wasn't quite sure he would ever take that step.

He liked his life the way it was. He liked the excitement of the track, the excitement of a new lover in his bed whenever he chose, and the excitement of creating something that would make him richer than he'd ever dreamed possible when he'd still been an angry teenager with a grudge against the world.

In short, he liked the freedom to do what he wished. He always made it clear to the women who got involved with him there was no future with him, and he didn't see that changing anytime soon.

Faith said he'd misread her last night, but he was certain he had not. She'd wanted him, and if he'd swept her into his arms and carried her to the bed, he was fairly certain she would not have objected. If he'd done so, he could be buried inside her right now instead of sitting at his desk and fighting an erection that wouldn't go away.

Renzo glanced down at the report that she'd handed him an hour ago, and then back up at where Faith sat at a desk nearby, clicking keys on her computer and generally ignoring him. He couldn't seem to concentrate on anything other than her. It was quite annoying.

If he had sex with her, she would leave him—but perhaps that was the lesser of two evils at this point since he needed to turn his attention to the next few months on the circuit and couldn't seem to do so.

He let his eyes skim down her form. Her hair was perfectly coiffed this morning, and she wore a cinnamon-colored jacket and skirt that showed off her legs. Gone were the unfashionable short black heels; in their place was a pair of platform pumps in brown suede. Faith had her legs tucked to one side of her chair, one lovely leg crossed over the other.

Thank God she had not looked like this in New York.

He'd been insane to take her to a salon, even more insane to take her shopping afterward. He'd known she was beautiful beneath the ill-fitting suits and glasses and severe buns, but he'd made a mistake in showcasing that beauty for others to see.

For Niccolo Gavretti to see. Renzo's grip tightened on the pen he was holding until he threw it down in disgust before it cracked. Gavretti had tried to kiss her and it had made him crazy. Crazy enough to mark her as his at a party attended by everyone who was anyone. Soon, the story would appear in the tabloids that regularly reported on his life. He had a feeling that Faith wouldn't like that, but there wasn't much he could do about it now.

She must have sensed he was looking at her because her head snapped up, her eyes meeting his evenly. But then she glanced down, just for a moment, and he knew she was still thinking about it, too.

"How is Lola this morning?" he asked, thinking of the tiny ball of fur that he'd found in the bougainvillea. The little thing had clawed him something fierce until she'd realized he wasn't going to hurt her. He had scratch marks on his arms this morning, and one on his chest.

"She's fine," Faith said. "I think she'll be able to eat kitten food if I can go and buy her some today."

Renzo waved a hand. "Consider it done," he said, picking up his mobile phone and calling Fabrizio, the household butler. "Anything else?" he asked while he still had the man on the phone.

"A proper litter box, litter, a playhouse—maybe I should just make a list."

"I will wait," he said, and Faith began to scribble on a piece of paper. She handed it over and Renzo read off the items to Fabrizio, who took everything in his stride. *Dio,* who knew one tiny creature needed so many things?

When he hung up again, she was watching him. "I forget sometimes just how exalted a life you lead," she said. "When was the last time you shopped for yourself?"

Renzo laughed. "I can't remember, *cara*. When I want something, I make a call. It is much more preferable to the way I used to live."

"And how was that? Like the rest of us mortals?" She was teasing him, and he found he liked it. She was trying so hard to make everything seem normal again. Did he want to give that up by taking her to his bed? He was very afraid he did.

"There was a time," he said, "when I didn't always have enough money to buy food for the day. It's amazing what you will do when you're hungry."

Her eyes filled with sadness, and he realized he'd said more than he'd meant to say. That was what he got for only having half his mind on the question and the other half on her legs.

"I'm sorry, Renzo. I know what it's like to worry about where your next meal is coming from. I wouldn't wish that on anyone."

His senses sharpened at the unhappy note in her voice. "When did this happen to you, Faith?"

She pushed back from her desk and folded her arms. The movement pressed her already lush breasts even higher. Renzo stifled a groan.

"I left home without much of a plan. It was inevitable there would be some difficulties along the way." She shook her head. "But I don't really want to talk about it. I shouldn't have brought it up."

"You never want to talk about it," he said, suddenly wanting to know more about her. What did he know, other than she was from Georgia, that she didn't speak to her family, and that she had a cat that'd died last year?

Her eyes flashed. "Neither do you," she accused. "We both tap-dance around the difficult parts of our lives. And maybe that's best. You're my boss, not my boyfriend."

At that moment, he wanted to be more. He wanted to be the man she told her problems to. The one whose arms she lay in at night before going to sleep.

Dio, this was insane. Renzo shoved back from the desk and stood. There was only one place he was going to stop thinking about her, at least for a little while. It would only be temporary, but temporary was better than nothing.

"If you're finished with your work for the morning, it's time to go to the track, *cara*."

Something else flashed in her eyes then—fear? Inexplicably, it made him angry. There was nothing to be frightened of. He knew what he was doing. He was Lorenzo D'Angeli. He'd won nine world titles, broken records—and shattered his leg.

He tightened his fingers into fists at his side. Yes, he'd shattered his leg. And yes, it was bothering him more and more lately. But it was time to take the Viper out and see how it rode now that they'd made the modifications. He wouldn't push it today, but he had to get a feel for it before training began in earnest.

"You want me to go with you?" she asked in disbelief.

"*Si*, I need you there."

She swallowed and turned around to log off her computer. Then she gathered her purse and stood. She didn't ask why he needed her to come with him and for that he was grateful. Because he couldn't give her a reason, other than he simply wanted her to be there.

He turned to go but she stopped him with a word.

"Renzo," she said, and he turned back to her. Her green

eyes were wide, her cheeks flushed. "I want you to promise me that if your leg starts to bother you, you won't push yourself," she said, clutching her purse in front of her like a shield. "It's not worth the risk."

He took a step closer to her, stopped. "Would you be upset if something happened to me, *cara*?"

"A lot of people would," she said, her lashes dipping to cover her eyes. "A lot of people depend on you."

"But would *you* be upset?"

He wasn't sure she would look at him, but she lifted her chin and met his gaze. "Yes, of course I would."

Some feeling he couldn't name curled inside him, warming him. "Then I suppose I will have to be careful."

If this was his idea of careful, then Faith wanted to scream. He'd taken her to a test track near the D'Angeli factory where she'd accompanied him as he'd inspected the Viper before suiting up and taking the beast out.

The motorcycle was wicked, with its cool carbon frame and cherry-red paint. It was wide in the front and narrow in the back, and didn't look at all like something any sane person would want to ride at the speeds Grand Prix racers rode. While the men had oohed and ahhed, she'd chewed the inside of her lip until it was nearly raw.

What if his leg cramped? What if he had an accident? What if, what if, what if?

Renzo had spent time conferring with his team before he'd gone to change. When he'd returned, he was clad head to toe in dark leather. It wasn't the leather he wore when racing, which was covered with logos and advertising, but it was still familiar from the photos she'd seen of him in his gear. He was wearing the knee sliders, the gloves, the lightweight boots and, when he turned to the side, the hump of the back protector was clearly visible.

She'd stood quietly by until he'd told someone to take her to the observation box. She'd stared at him, wanting to say something, until she'd finally had to turn and follow the man who was taking her away.

Now, she sat in the box and clenched her hands into tight fists as Renzo raced along a track that curved up high on the sides and contained at least one switchback, which he regularly took at lightning speed.

The motorcycle roared into the curves—and that's when Faith couldn't breathe. She'd watched footage of the races previously, because she'd felt it necessary if she was working at D'Angeli Motors, but she'd never before thought she was going to scream each time the motorcycle lay flat on its side, Renzo's knee and elbow skimming the ground before it came out on the other side and he throttled it higher, zooming into hyper speeds.

It was, without doubt, the most insane thing she'd ever witnessed—and that was going some, considering she was from the American South and car racing was a favored sport of many people there. But no car race she'd ever been forced to watch with her family could compare to the outright insanity of this.

When Renzo finally finished his run in what seemed like a century later, she wilted in relief. He brought the motorcycle to a stop, though not until after doing a series of wheelies, and climbed off as someone prepared to take the bike from him.

What happened next brought a gasp from her companions in the box—and sent her racing down the stairs as fast as she could go in her high heels.

The instant Renzo's right foot had touched the tarmac, he'd buckled into a heap.

By the time she reached ground level and burst out onto the track, he was standing and shaking his head as someone said something to him. He'd raised the visor on his helmet, but now he removed it and laid it on the seat as she barreled toward him.

Faith stopped short as several pairs of eyes turned toward her, questioning. But it was the look in Renzo's eyes that most concerned her. There was pain, she could clearly see that, but he was doing his best to hide it. Not only that, but he glared daggers at her. A warning.

"I beg your pardon," she said, even though her heart raced and a fine sheen of sweat broke out between her breasts. She had to salvage this somehow, had to help him out of the situation. "But, uh, you have an important conference call scheduled quite soon, Mr. D'Angeli. I thought you might have forgotten it in the excitement of testing the, uh, the Viper."

He stared at her for a long moment. "Thank you, Miss Black."

He turned back to the men and said a few things in Italian, and then he was moving toward her, no trace of a limp as he strode with the confidence and surety that she was accustomed to seeing in him.

But she could tell he was hurting. The corners of his mouth were tight and there was a groove in his forehead as he concentrated hard on walking without letting the pain show. They swept into the factory and then took an elevator up to his office. Once inside, he still didn't give in to the agony he was surely feeling. He walked over to his desk and sat down, his body still encased in racing leather.

And then he folded over until his head was on his arms and she could hear him breathing deeply.

"Renzo," she said, choking back tears as she went to his side and sank down beside him. "What can I do?"

"Nothing," he said. "There is nothing."

She reached up with shaking fingers and touched his

sweat-soaked hair. "I'm sorry. I seem to say that quite a lot, but I don't know what else to say." She let her hand drop to his shoulder, squeezed. "I think you should take a pain pill. And then you should call your doctor."

"No doctors," he said. "No pills."

Frustration pounded into her. "You can't just endure it," she said, trying to reason with him. "At least take a pill."

He pushed himself upright and her heart twisted as she got a look at him. His eyes were glazed, as if he'd been on the edge of tears.

"Does it hurt that badly?"

He gave a poor imitation of a laugh. "Worse."

Faith swallowed the lump in her throat. "Please consider taking a pain pill."

"Give me some of those pills from your purse," he said. "Maybe that will do the trick."

She didn't think so, but she dutifully complied, finding bottled water in the refrigerator built into the sleek counter on one wall. He'd removed his gloves by the time she returned to him, and he took the pills, draining half the water, then leaned back in his chair, one hand spanning his forehead as he sat with his eyes closed.

"How was the Viper to ride?" she asked. "Was it everything you'd hoped?"

He actually smiled. "It was glorious, *cara mia*. Almost perfect. There are a few tweaks required, but she'll be ready to go when it's time."

"I'm glad to hear it." Except, of course, Renzo would insist on riding the motorcycle himself instead of giving it to one of the racing team to ride. "What happened when you got off the Viper, Renzo?"

She wasn't sure he would tell her, but then he sighed. "My leg started to cramp on the final few laps. And that last turn was a bit hard on the knee. The pain was…surprising, I suppose."

"You promised not to push it," she said tightly. "I wish you would at least see a doctor. He might be able to help."

His blue eyes were piercing when they snapped open. "No. I've seen doctors. There is nothing they can tell me that I do not already know."

"Do you really think you can ride the Viper for an entire season? How will you explain it if you can't stand up when they hand you the trophy?" She could think of far worse scenarios, but she couldn't bring herself to say them. He knew the possibilities as well as she did.

His voice was as hard as diamonds. "I can ride, Faith. There is no other choice."

She swallowed the fear and bitterness roiling in her belly. "I don't understand that, Renzo. You have an entire racing team at your disposal. Men who know how this is done as well as you do."

"They don't know," he snapped, before muttering something in Italian. "I am one of the top-ranked riders in the world. And I know my motorcycles. It has to be me. This is the Viper's debut. It has to succeed, and for that to happen, I must be the one riding. The sponsors are counting on it. The company is counting on it. Do you wish to find yourself downsized because the Viper fails?"

She knew how much it meant to him, how proud he was, and yet she didn't believe it was as dire as he made it out to be. Yes, they might lose sponsors and, yes, the newest production model might not sell as well as hoped if the Viper was a disaster. Gavretti Manufacturing might even gain the upper hand on them, which would no doubt anger Renzo a great deal.

But so what? He would be alive and able to bring the company back from the edge of whatever misfortune they might teeter upon. "D'Angeli isn't going to go broke if the Viper doesn't smash records," Faith said firmly.

He looked at her darkly for several moments. And then he stood, his face whitening briefly as he clutched the edge of the desk. "I'll shower and change and then we can go back to the villa."

Faith ground her teeth in frustration. Typical man. He didn't want to talk about it when she pointed out the flaws in his logic.

He started to limp toward the adjoining bath, but she hurried over and slid an arm around his waist. He might be stubborn, but she couldn't watch him suffer.

"*Grazie*," he said, leaning on her as she helped him into the bathroom. It was a luxurious room, outfitted in exotic African hardwoods and sleek chrome fixtures. There was a huge shower at one end, entirely encased in glass, complete with a bench and several nozzles up and down the walls on three sides, as well as one overhead.

"Sit," she told him when they reached the leather couch in the dressing area off to one side.

He did as she said, and then she bent to take his boots off even though he had not asked her to. But how could he manage it when his leg still hurt? She got one boot off, and then the other before tackling the knee sliders, which were separate from the leathers because they had to be replaced so often. These were scraped pretty badly from his contact with the track, and it made her shudder to think again of how he lay almost flat on his side every time he went around a curve.

The barest slip of control and he and the bike would go their separate ways. At two hundred miles an hour.

Faith shuddered again. The leathers were made for protection, with Kevlar and titanium in the most vulnerable spots, but the last thing she wanted was to see firsthand how good the protection they provided was.

How was it that one of the other talented riders on the D'Angeli team couldn't ride the Viper? She didn't believe it for a moment, no matter how good Renzo was. With Renzo as a teacher, how could his team fail? He was simply too proud, too stubborn, to admit he couldn't do this any longer.

She got the sliders off and then lifted her head to look at him. The last thing she expected to see was the jut of an impressive arousal against the leather. Her gaze flew to his.

He smiled crookedly. "I could see down your shirt," he said, not the least bit apologetic. "It's a nice view."

"You're in no shape to be thinking about my breasts," she told him somewhat prudishly, her cheeks flaring with heat.

He laughed. "*Cara*, I'd have to be dead not to think about your breasts. I assure you I'm quite capable of thinking about them. Of thinking of every centimeter of your body, I should add."

Faith got to her feet and stood stiffly, in spite of the fact her body was doing that softening-melting-aching thing again. "I think you can do the rest yourself," she said. "I'll wait in the office."

He stood, his face less tight now, and tugged at the zipper that held the leathers in place. It was like having that magazine ad come to life, she thought, as her breath caught and held while the zipper slid downward. Unlike in the magazine, there was a tight shirt beneath the leather, but it was still one of the sexiest things she'd ever seen.

"I'll be, um, in the office," she said, turning away as he laughed.

"You could stay, Faith. Wash my back."

She spun to face him again just as he shrugged out of

the top half of the leathers and then peeled the shirt up and off. She'd seen his naked chest last night, but it had been dark. Now he stood before her in all his hard-bodied glory, muscles rippling and flexing beneath bronzed skin—and then she noticed a three-pronged scratch skating over one pectoral muscle.

Faith frowned even as her heart did that funny little skip thing again. She thought of him last night with a tiny mewing bundle in his arms. "Lola did that?"

He glanced down. "*Si*—but it is nothing."

And then he was staring at her again, blue eyes daring her. Only a few minutes ago, he'd been in enough pain to bring tears to his eyes, and now he was standing there like some sexy demigod and tempting her into the kind of behavior that ought to make her turn and run right this instant. Instead, she was imagining it. Considering it.

Wanting it.

"How about it, Faith?" he said, his voice a sexy rumble. "Do you want to wash my back?"

"I—I—" She closed her eyes, darted her tongue over her lips. She was not doing this. She was not stripping her clothing and stepping into that shower with him when he'd probably done the same thing a million times before with a million different women. She couldn't. "I'll be in the office, Renzo."

Before he could say another word, she hurried out the door and shut it firmly behind her. But his laughter echoed after her until she almost turned around and went back just so she could look at him one more time. Instead, she retreated to a chair by the window and forced herself to sit with her hands in her lap and stare at the Tuscan hills.

He emerged twenty minutes later, dressed in the trousers and button-down shirt he'd worn earlier, his hair still damp and curling sexily over his collar. Faith stood, clasping her hands together to hide their trembling. Her heart was still racing, and her body still ached, no matter that she'd sat and tried to will the feelings away.

It didn't work that way, apparently. She wanted things she'd never wanted before, and she didn't quite know how to get them. How to take that plunge that would mean the difference between continuing the way she had been, and knowing what it meant to be a sensual creature focused on her own pleasure.

Renzo stopped when he saw her. His gaze met hers, heat flaring anew in the blue depths, and she knew that he could see her struggle with herself. He was far too perceptive when it came to women. She tried to remind herself why that was a bad thing, but she just didn't seem to care.

"Come here, Faith," he said, and she obeyed without once asking herself why she was doing so. He smelled delicious, clean and fresh and male, and she itched to touch him. But she kept her arms rigid at her sides as she stood before him and waited for something to happen.

Until he reached for her and tugged her into his embrace. One hand came up to cup her jaw while the other spread across the small of her back, pressing her to him. Faith gripped the powerful muscles of his biceps, her breath shortening in her chest.

"I've been thinking about something," he said as she blinked up at him and wondered how any man could be so absolutely stunning. "I can't stop thinking about it, in fact."

"What's that?" she asked, trying not to devolve into a stammering idiot.

He smiled, and her stomach flipped. "I want to be your first, Faith."

She blinked. "M-my first?"

First what? She couldn't think, simply couldn't form a thought in her head when he held her so close, his body warm and hard against hers, his mouth so close, so sexy that she wanted to bite him, kiss him, lick him.

He dipped his head until those perfect lips were only a whisper away from hers.

"Yes, *cara mia,* I want to be your first lover."

She would never be certain who moved first, but then his lips were on hers and she was lost.

CHAPTER NINE

FAITH melted into his kiss as if she'd been born to do so. No man had ever kissed her the way Renzo had, she thought crazily. He kissed the way he rode motorcycles: expertly, passionately, and with a combination of control and recklessness that slayed her ability to think rationally about anything.

She was lost, helpless, powerless to resist when he held her so close, his mouth slanting over hers, his tongue sliding and teasing and tormenting.

He kissed her until she moaned, kissed her until she wrapped her arms around him and arched her body against his. Until she forgot who she was or where she was or why this might possibly turn out badly for her in the end.

His hand slid down her body, brought her hips in contact with his, and she gasped at the evidence of his need for her.

"I want you, Faith," he said in her ear. "But I want you to make the choice. It has nothing to do with who we are, and everything to do with this raw need we both feel when we touch. I want to explore this feeling, and I want to show you how good it can be between us when we do."

She could no longer deny that she wanted it, too. "Not here," she said quickly. "I don't want to do it here."

He lifted his head until he could look down at her, stroked his fingers over her cheek before tucking her hair

behind her ear. "Of course not," he said. "Tell me what
your fantasy is, *cara*. A castle? A desert tent? A tropical
island? Name it, and it's yours."

Her pulse thrummed in her throat until she felt dizzy,
drunk with passion and happiness and fear all at once.

"I—I've never quite thought about it." My God, what
was she agreeing to? Was she really going to be this man's
lover? Was she really negotiating the terms of her surrender in a sunlit office in Tuscany?

"What about Venice?" he said. "A gorgeous palazzo on
the Grand Canal. I will do this for you, Faith, if it's what
you want."

He looked so serious, and she knew that no matter what
she named, no matter how far-fetched, he would move
heaven and earth to get it for her. To make her first time
special. She was touched that he would go to such trouble,
and yet at this moment she wanted none of those things.

She only wanted him. In a bed. In his villa, with the
scents of the flowers on the breeze and his taste on her
tongue. That was all she needed to make it special, mem-
orable.

But she felt unsophisticated for wanting something so
simple when he was offering her the world. Would he think
her too sentimental if she told him? Too unimaginative?

"I can see that you've thought of something," he said.
"But you do not want to tell me. What is it, *cara*? Do you
wish to refuse my offer? It is your choice, as I have said."

Faith sighed and lifted her hand to trace her fingers
across his full lower lip. She was beyond hope now. She
couldn't refuse even if her life depended on it. She knew
that her heart probably depended on it, but that couldn't
stop her, either.

Her fingers moved back and forth while he held completely still. She'd never done anything so sensual or bold

to a man in her life, and yet the darkening of his eyes told her he liked it. She liked it, too. She felt as if there was a thread running from her fingers to her core, and when she touched him, her sex tightened with need.

"I want to go back to the villa, Renzo."

He captured her fingers in his and kissed them. "Then that is where we shall go."

The villa was only a short car ride away, but by the time they arrived, her bravado was fading and nerves were taking over. She was about to let a famous heartbreaker make love to her for the first time in her life. What if he didn't enjoy it? What if he was disappointed?

Because this wasn't about love. It was about desire and heat, about sexual gratification. Things that she knew nothing about, or at least not yet. What if she was terrible at it?

They left the car in the drive and passed into the house through the kitchen door, which was open to the breeze and the bright afternoon sunshine. The cook, Lucia, was busy making something that smelled wonderful. She looked up when they entered, and smiled. Renzo spoke to her for a few moments before Faith followed him into the long hallway leading toward the grand staircase, butterflies swirling in her belly until she was nearly sick with it.

When they were almost at the stairs, Renzo caught her to him and her blood began to sing once again. If he would just hold her, she could do anything.

"I want you desperately, *cara mia*," he said, his blue eyes serious as he studied her face, "but I want you to be certain. And I want to do this right. You should be wined and dined and seduced, not taken upstairs and stripped naked simply for my pleasure."

She clutched his sleeves as he cupped her face. She waited for the perfect storm of his kiss, that melding of lips and tongues that drove her insane with need, but his lips only skimmed hers, the kiss chaste and soft. When she would have wrapped her arms around his neck and pulled him to her, he lifted his head.

"Go, before I lose the will to send you away. We will dine together at eight. What happens then is entirely up to you."

It was nearly ten minutes after eight when she walked into the dining room. Renzo turned at the sound of her entrance. He'd been convinced she'd changed her mind when she hadn't been prompt—Faith had never been late even a single day at work, so it was inconceivable that she could be late now unless she wasn't joining him on purpose.

But she was here, and his blood began to hum at the sight of her. It was true he didn't know if she'd changed her mind or not, but the way she was dressed gave him hope. She wore a body-skimming blue wrap dress that was more daring than anything he'd yet seen her wear. It was still modest—Faith would always be modest—but the dress dipped in a V that showed the barest hint of cleavage while clinging to her curves.

Curves he wanted to explore in thorough detail.

Her color was high, he noted, her green eyes wide. Her blond hair spilled freely down her back, silky and shining in the lights from the Murano chandelier overhead. He had a sudden visceral reaction: he wanted to bury his fingers in her hair while he thrust into her body again and again.

Santo cielo.

He'd been determined not to do this, not to give in to his desire for her now that he knew she was a virgin. But he'd realized today, when she'd bent down to remove his boots, that she was a fire in his blood he wasn't going to quench any other way. Hell, she'd even invaded his ride on the Viper. At a time when he most needed his concentration, she'd been in his head, her pretty eyes and flushed cheeks, her beautiful full breasts, her hot little tongue as he'd kissed her in the car last night.

Faith was in his blood, in his body, and he knew of no other way to drive her out than to immerse himself in her. But the choice was hers. Only hers. He would not take advantage of her innocence. If she told him to go to hell, then he would find another woman tomorrow and take care of this burning sexual need at the least.

"I'm sorry I'm late," she said a touch breathlessly. "Lola wouldn't settle down."

"And how is our tiny tyrant?" he asked, going over and pulling out her chair like a gentleman instead of staring at her like the slavering beast he was. She skimmed past him, her hair brushing his arm, her sweet scent wrapping around his senses. She smelled like vanilla, he realized. Soft, warm vanilla.

It reminded him of home. Of his early home, when he was still a small child and his mother had plenty of work— and plenty of male attention, though he'd not known or cared how important that was to her then. They'd had a nice apartment with a sliver of a sea view. It had been tiny, but his memories of it were warm and happy.

Faith laughed as she sat down, though the sound was a bit high and nervous. Not the sound of a woman who planned to say no. Possessive heat coiled in his belly even as he felt a twinge of guilt.

"She is very tiny, and very tyrannical," Faith said, and he remembered that they had been talking of Lola. "But so adorable."

He took his seat, determined to do this right. To make this night special for her. "You love her already."

She smiled. "I do. It's hard not to. That's why Mother Nature makes babies so cute."

"Then I did the right thing in giving her to you." It gave him pleasure to see her smile. He'd rarely seen her smile in all the time she'd worked for him. She was always so serious, so proper.

She met his gaze then, and he could see the worry in her expression. "How is your leg, Renzo? Was it just a cramp, or did you reinjure it on the track today?"

Something inside him tightened. "I did not injure myself, *cara*."

She let out a sigh. "I'm glad."

A lot of people would be glad he wasn't injured—his team, his stockholders, his mother and sister—but somehow it seemed more important that she was relieved. That the worry lining her face was even now smoothing out and disappearing.

The meal arrived then, and their talk was confined to things like the kitten, his run on the track today—without any further mention of a doctor or his difficulty at the end of the ride, *grazie a Dio*—and the beauty of the Tuscan countryside.

"I will take you to Florence soon," he told her, and she smiled so genuinely that it actually hurt. She was so sweet and innocent, and he had no right to take her for his own when he did not intend to keep her.

He should get up now, get into his car and go to his apartment in Florence. Alone.

But he would not. He wasn't that selfless.

"Can we see *David*?" she asked excitedly.

"Of course. He is quite magnificent. I am an Italian male, and yet the first time I saw him, even I was moved by the beauty of the sculpture."

She sighed. "There is so much beauty in Italy."

"*Si*," he said meaningfully. "There is."

Her lashes dropped. She reached for her wineglass, her fingers trembling. It nearly undid him.

"Faith."

She looked up. "Yes?"

"You can say no." He drew in a deep breath. He couldn't believe what he was about to say. "You probably should say no, *cara*. I offer you nothing except pleasure. And you can wait for that when the time—and the man—is right."

She dipped her head to study the wine in her glass, tucking a lock of hair behind her ear as she did so. "If you don't want me, it's okay. I understand. I'm not sophisticated or experienced enough for a man like you, and maybe it is better if we continue to be professional after all."

He reached across the table to tip her chin up. She tried to keep her eyes from meeting his. "Look at me," he commanded.

Her lashes lifted until he was staring into the deepest, greenest eyes he'd ever seen. He felt a jolt in his gut, a visceral need for her that stunned him with its intensity.

"What I want is you beneath me. Naked, *cara mia*. Right now would not be soon enough."

There was an electrical current in the air, sliding between them on invisible pathways that sparked and sizzled with each look, each touch, that flowed between them. Faith's blood felt hot, thick, and her chest ached as if she couldn't quite breathe properly.

Anticipation coiled in her belly. *Naked*. She tried to imagine it, tried to imagine what he said he wanted, and her vision swam as she did so.

She could hear Renzo's soft laugh, and then he was standing and pulling her to her feet, holding her close. "Breathe, Faith. Don't pass out on me."

She clutched her fingers into the expensive silk of his

shirt and sucked air into her lungs. Air that smelled like him, spicy and male and clean.

"You must think me ridiculous," she said, her voice muffled against his chest.

He stroked her hair. "Not at all. I think you're refreshing. Lovely."

"This is not quite how I imagined my first time would go."

His voice was smooth, warm. "And what did you imagine, *cara*?"

She shrugged. She'd imagined love, though she wouldn't tell him that. She wasn't naive—she was a grown woman who'd had to take care of herself for the past eight years. She'd had roommates, she'd watched movies and she'd listened to bedroom tales when her roommates wanted to share. But, through it all, she'd imagined some sort of special moment when Faith Black—Faith Winston—met her Prince Charming. The man who would love her the way she loved him, and who would pledge his soul to hers when he made love to her for the first time.

It was a crazy fantasy, a girlish fantasy. She knew better. Relationships were messy and imperfect, and you kissed a lot of frogs before you found Prince Charming.

"I'm not sure," she said softly. "Music, dancing, candles. Romantic nonsense."

"It's not nonsense if it's what you want." He took her hand and led her into the living area. The room was beautiful, she thought wistfully, as she sat on the plush couch at his direction and let her eyes roam over the wood beams and the original artwork that graced the stuccoed walls. Renzo picked up a remote control, and then the soft strains of smooth jazz filled the background.

There were candles clustered in the hearth, she realized, when he struck a long match and lit them. Then he returned to the couch and sat beside her. She thought he might pull her into his arms, kiss her, but he simply sat back and put his arm around her. After a moment's hesitation, she curled into him and watched the flames.

"Do you want me to tell you about my first time?" he asked.

Faith nodded. She could feel his smile against her temple. "This is top secret information, *cara*. It would surely ruin me if it got out."

"I doubt that."

He laughed at the sarcasm in her voice. "I was seventeen," he said. "And very green. She was older than I, so sexy and experienced that I could not believe she wanted me."

"I can," Faith said, and meant it.

"Nevertheless, I fumbled quite badly. She was very patient."

Faith pushed back until she could see his face. "What do you mean, fumbled?"

His blue eyes were sharp. Sexy. She could drown in those eyes. "I mean that I failed. That I lasted about as long as it takes the Viper to go from zero to one hundred."

Faith could only blink.

"Don't look so surprised," he said.

"But you did it right the second time."

He nodded. "The second time was about fifteen minutes later. It was quite an improvement."

"You're only saying this to make me feel better. You didn't really, um…"

"Come too quickly? I did." He dipped his head and kissed her, his voice a soft, sensual growl when next he spoke. "I assure you this is no longer a problem."

Faith strained toward him, even though she was already close. She wanted him to kiss her again, to kiss her the way he had in his office, to make her forget everything but him and this moment together. Her body hummed with excitement, with anticipation and nerves and a zillion other feelings that were sparking and zapping inside her.

So long as he kissed her, the fear was submersed beneath the need.

One hand spanned her jaw, and then his mouth slanted over hers again, taking her roughly. She was shocked—and aroused. She wanted this kiss, wanted it just like this. Because it reminded her of last night, in the car, when he'd seemed so barely controlled that she'd thought he would tear her clothes off and make her his in a too-small sports car parked in the Tuscan countryside.

"Faith," he murmured. "You are so sweet. So intoxicating. Why did I not realize this before?"

"Renzo." His name was a sigh.

His lips touched hers again, and then his tongue slid against hers like silk and she moaned. She knew the rhythm so well now. Knew it as if she'd been born to kiss this one particular man for eternity.

She expected that he would quickly tire of the kissing and try to move on to the main event. That's what Jason had done on the fateful night when she'd refused him. She'd felt so badly afterward that she'd committed the single biggest error of her life.

Tonight, however, was not an error. She was twenty-six, more than responsible for herself—and more than ready to experience lovemaking.

Renzo kissed her endlessly, tirelessly, as if he had all night to do so. The tension in her body wound tighter and tighter until she throbbed with it. She wanted him so badly that it hurt—physically hurt—not to have him.

She was on fire. She wanted her clothes off, wanted to feel the cool air wafting over her sweat-sheened skin.

Renzo must have sensed it, because he stood then and pulled her with him. Without a word, they climbed the stairs to the second floor, where he tugged her into his arms and kissed her even while he moved her inexorably toward her bedroom.

A moment later, he scooped her up and carried her into the room—not hers, she realized, but his. This room was even bigger than the one she was staying in, and furnished with antiques, priceless art and a large bed with white linens that he laid her on before coming down over top of her.

Faith wrapped her arms around his neck, arched her body toward his. His arousal came as no surprise, considering the way she felt. He was big, hard, and he moved his hips against hers until she caught fire. Her body spiraled toward the peak, but he did not let her reach it. Before she fell over the edge, he stopped, moved down her body, kissed her throat, the exposed skin at the top of her dress.

Then he lifted himself onto his knees and shrugged out of his shirt while she bit her lip and stared. His eyes were so hot, so full of promise, as he gazed down on her.

"You could not have chosen a sexier dress, Faith," he said, his voice rough. His fingers strayed to the tie at her waist. "You wrapped yourself up for me, and I've been looking forward to the unwrapping all night."

CHAPTER TEN

Renzo tugged at the knot at her waist until it came free. Faith held her breath as he undid the inner knot—and then he opened the dress as if he were opening a present, his eyes gleaming appreciatively as they slid over her.

She'd never been so open to a man in her life, and yet she didn't feel exposed. She felt beautiful, desirable. She didn't envy the Katie Palmers of the world at this moment. No, it was they who should envy her. Because this gorgeous, gorgeous man was looking at her like she was the only one in the world who could satisfy him.

It might only be temporary, might only be for this one moment in time, but she didn't care. Right now, he was hers. She could see it in his eyes, in his beautiful masculine body. His entire focus was on her, and she knew she wouldn't be the same after tonight.

Renzo shook his head slowly. "What have you been hiding from me, Faith? For six long months, you've been hiding this sexy body."

He made her blush. "At this point, I'm a sure thing," she said, her heart beating hard. "You don't have to flatter me to get your way."

He looked so serious. "It is not flattery, Faith. It's truth. You are incredibly sexy." He spread his hand over her belly.

It wasn't a flat belly, not like his, and she bit her lip as embarrassment sliced through her.

"Renzo—"

"I love your skin," he told her, as if she hadn't spoken. "So creamy and pale. And your curves." He sucked in a breath. "*Dio*, Faith, your curves could kill a man if he weren't careful."

His hand slid down over her hip, skimmed over the silk of her panties, and then back up to cup a breast. His other hand went behind her back, unsnapped her bra, and then he was lifting it off her arms—along with the dress—and tossing it aside.

"They aren't perfect," Faith blurted. "They aren't round and perky and firm."

Renzo put a finger over her lips. "Don't talk, *cara mia*. Feel."

He bent until his mouth hovered over one stiff nipple. "I love your breasts. They are real. Round and firm, as you say, is usually made of silicone."

He licked the tip of her nipple, and her sex tightened. "Renzo," she gasped.

"Yes, *amore, feel*."

He made love to her nipples then, licking and sucking the stiff little points until she wanted to scream. She'd never known that arousal could be painful until tonight. Because she burned for more than this, exquisite as it was. She burned for his body inside hers, for the sweetness of a shattering climax. She was gasping with need, writhing beneath him, and still he wouldn't put her out of her misery.

When he moved down her body, his mouth skimming her flesh, she cried out. If this was what making love felt like, why had she waited so long?

Because this was what making love with *Renzo* felt like. It would not have been the same with another man.

He tugged her panties from her hips, sliding them from her legs, and then he brought her to his mouth and slid his tongue along the seam of her sex. She arched up off the bed when he did so, her entire body on fire in a way she'd never before experienced. Of course she'd had self-induced orgasms before, but she'd never felt this kind of *excitement* in the buildup.

Renzo spread her with his thumbs. The instant his tongue touched her soft, sensitive core, she came apart with a cry. The sensations had been building for so long, her body growing so tight with it, that she needed nothing else to send her plunging over the edge. He didn't take his mouth off her as she shattered. Instead, he pushed her harder over the edge, kept the pressure focused on that one spot, his tongue darting and swirling long after she would have thought she had nothing left.

When it was over, she closed her eyes and turned her head into the pillow. Embarrassment echoed through her. And something else. Something hot and dark and ecstatic.

And yet she was surprised to realize that she wasn't completely satisfied. She felt boneless, liquid—and edgy. There was more, so much more that she'd not yet experienced.

"*Dio*, you are sexy," Renzo said, his voice roughened with passion. "The things I want to do to you, Faith. You tempt me beyond what is reasonable."

She couldn't speak as he stood and stripped off his trousers. She could only watch as his body was revealed inch by delicious inch, her breath catching in her chest at the sight of Renzo D'Angeli finally in the very naked and very hot flesh.

He knelt between her legs. He was big and hard and beautiful, and her heart thrummed so fast it made her dizzy. She reached for him, wanting to touch that part of him she knew nothing about. She'd never seen a man naked in the flesh before, and he fascinated her.

His breath hissed in as she tentatively stroked her fingers along his erection. He *was* hot. And very hard.

"Wrap your hand around me," he said, and she obeyed. She could feel him pulsing beneath her palm. It made her feel powerful, sexy, to know she'd caused this reaction. He put his hand over hers, showed her how to stroke him. When he let her go, she didn't stop. Boldly, she continued to stroke him, loving the way he groaned. A second later, he pulled her hand away, kissing her fingertips.

"Much more of that," he told her, "and it will be like *my* first time again."

He was far too experienced to lose control that easily, and yet it made her heart soar to think she could excite him that much.

He grabbed a condom from the nightstand and sheathed himself. Still kneeling, he lifted her hips and positioned himself at her entrance.

"If it hurts too much, you must tell me," he said.

She nodded, and then the hot, hard head of him was pushing into her. It was a tight fit, but it didn't hurt quite the way she'd expected it would.

"You are so ready for me," he said, his voice unexpectedly raw, his eyes closing tight as the muscles in his neck corded.

He didn't move for a long minute, and then he lowered himself on top of her. His mouth slanted over hers as he thrust completely inside her. Faith gasped at the fullness of his possession, at the heat and light shimmering through her, at this feeling of finally being joined with him. But there was no tearing, no pain.

Renzo lifted his head to look at her curiously.

"It happened at the doctor's office," she blurted, suddenly worried he might think she'd lied about being a virgin when there was no hymen. "My first exam."

His thumbs glided over her cheeks as he held himself still while she got used to the feel of him inside her. "You are the most surprising woman, Faith…."

"You believe me," she said softly, her body trembling from nerves and excitement. She hadn't much considered how he might react until the moment came. That he believed her without hesitation made her chest ache. It was more than her family had done for her when the picture she'd sent Jason went viral. They'd believed the worst from that moment onward.

"Of course I do," he said, dipping his head to run his tongue along her lower lip. "Why wouldn't I?"

Something inside her twisted. Faith glided her palms along the muscles of his arms, arching her body against him, shuddering as sensation rolled through her when he moved his hips just the tiniest bit. It was the most beautiful feeling.

And she wanted more of it. She wanted the physical so she could take her mind off the emotional, off the way he smashed all her misconceptions about him.

"Now," she said—begged, really, "please, now."

With a growl, he began to move, slowly at first, and then faster as she wrapped her legs around his waist and lifted her hips to meet him with every thrust.

It was a bold move, very unlike her in many ways, and yet she couldn't help herself. Because it was a revelation, this feeling of having a man inside her for the first time.

It was raw and sexy and primal, but it was also beautiful. Faith closed her eyes. She'd never felt so close to another person in her life, never felt so cherished and special.

Renzo bracketed her face in his hands and kissed her, a hot, wet kiss that excited her almost as much as his body possessing hers so completely did. She was spiraling higher, her body catching fire with feelings she'd never experienced.

When his mouth moved to her nipples, she couldn't keep her moans of pleasure locked inside any longer. She was losing control of herself—and she didn't care.

Her hips thrust up to meet his, her body accepting—demanding—the exquisite torment of his lovemaking. He answered her with an intensity she hadn't imagined possible. Their bodies moved together, lifting and sinking and soaring, until stars exploded behind her eyes and she cried out.

He kept moving, kept thrusting, wringing every last moment of pleasure from her until a ragged groan tore from his throat. And then he sank down on top of her, his mouth taking hers again, before he rolled to the side and pulled her with him.

Faith lay against him, panting, her body still tingling and shuddering in the aftermath.

My God, what had just happened to her? She'd never flown so completely apart, nor wanted the feeling so desperately that she would have done anything to get it.

Renzo's breathing was as hard as hers as his fingers skimmed down her naked back. A few moments later, he got up and walked into the attached bathroom, and her skin began to cool when he was no longer lying next to her. She lay sprawled on the bed, her body flushed and quivering and moist, and a sudden sensation of guilt pricked at her conscience.

She reached for the covers, suddenly acutely aware of her own nakedness. The room wasn't brightly lit, but a lamp was on, spilling soft light over the rumpled bed.

She was not like Renzo, she thought. He was so beautiful, so perfectly made, muscles bunching and rippling as he moved.

And she was softer than she should be, padded. She was definitely not underwear model material. She yanked the covers to her chin as the heat of embarrassment infused her. Renzo had been too preoccupied before to really notice the flaws in her body—but now? Now he would notice everything.

Faith would have shot from the bed and grabbed her clothes, but he returned too quickly. As he strode toward the bed, she got her first good look at his injured leg. There was a long scar down one side of his thigh and along the side of his knee. The scar was faded, but still noticeable.

He stopped and glanced down at his leg, and she realized she must have been frowning. She tried to wipe the look from her face, but he wasn't fooled.

"It was a long time ago," he said. "And yes, it was bad. So bad they said I would never race again."

Faith bit her lip. She hated to think of him in so much pain, being told he couldn't do the one thing he loved to do, the thing he had been the best in the world at. For the first time ever, she had an idea of just how hard he must have fought to prove them wrong. And how much it frustrated him to be dealing with it again now when he thought he'd conquered it.

"But that is unimportant at this moment," he said, joining her in the bed again. His fingers hooked into the covers and tugged gently. "Let me see you, Faith."

"You already saw me."

He laughed. "It's a little late for modesty, don't you think?"

Her ears burned. It was a little late for *everything*. Where was her decorum, her sense? Her self-respect? She'd tumbled headlong into carnality. If she was sorry now, it was no less than she deserved.

Except that she wasn't sorry. Not for what they'd done.

If she was sorry for anything, it was that she'd given herself to him and erased the mystery. How soon before he tired of her? How soon before she was looking for another job?

She'd done the one thing that she'd sworn she would never, ever do. She'd had sex with her billionaire boss, and become one of *those* women who seemed to think they could sleep their way to a better job or a better life. She knew women like that, women she'd met who worked for powerful men and thought that sleeping with them would lead to love.

Elaine had never admitted it, but Faith was convinced that's why her roommate left the city and returned to Ohio. She'd had an affair with a man in her office who, while not her boss, was in senior management and quite wealthy. And married, it turned out. The affair had been over for a while, but Elaine had never quite gotten over it.

Renzo leaned down and kissed her, and Faith's body started to melt. It surprised her, how she could respond so instantly after what they'd just done. She should be replete, too satisfied to react.

And yet she wasn't. It was a shock to realize that if he wanted her again, right now, she'd happily wrap herself around him and go along for the ride.

And it was terrifying, too. If she couldn't control herself now, what would happen later, when she was so accustomed to his lovemaking that the inevitable breakup would crush her? She'd be one of those pitiful women who kept calling his office—except that *she* was the gatekeeper.

Faith wanted to whimper and wail—and surrender to his touch.

Renzo was oblivious to the feelings crashing through her as he kissed her, and the covers inched down until she could feel the air sliding over her breasts, her torso.

"Beautiful," he said, his hot mouth kissing a trail to her breasts. "I think I should keep you naked at all times."

"It would make getting work done a little difficult," she said, trying hard to be sophisticated and cool.

He propped himself on an elbow, his gaze smoldering. "Not if you worked in here."

She reached for the covers again, and this time he did not stop her. "I—I think I should go back to my room now."

His brows lifted in surprise. And then drew down as his features clouded. "Why would you want to do that?"

She couldn't look at him. Her heart was pounding, her stomach flipping. What was she doing? "Thank you for showing me what it was like. For being my f-first. But I still work for you, and if I'm going to do my job properly, then I should go back to my own room now."

His face was a thundercloud. She didn't think she'd ever seen him so angry. Not even when Niccolo Gavretti had tried to kiss her. He swore in Italian—and then in English, shocking her with the coarseness of his words.

He shot from the bed and stood there in all his naked glory. "Fine. Go then."

Misery sliced into her. They'd been so close, and now she'd done this. She'd alienated him when all she wanted to do was turn into his arms and sleep the night away. "You need to turn around."

"No." His voice was hard, cruel. "We just had sex, Faith. I think I know what you look like. What you feel like. If you want to leave, get out of the bed and get dressed right now. I'm not going anywhere."

She hesitated a minute before climbing from the bed and dragging the top cover with her. Renzo wrapped his fists in it and stripped it away, forcing her to stand there naked and exposed.

Like he was.

She wrapped her arms around her torso, turning in a circle while she searched for her dress. It was on the other side of the bed. She went to get it but before she could bend down, he was there, jerking her into his arms, pressing the full length of her naked body against his.

"You don't want to go," he said harshly. "You're only doing this because you think you have to. Because you think I won't want you anymore. But I do, Faith. I *do*."

Faith shivered. Her hands were fists against his pectoral muscles, her forearms resting against his chest. And she was softening inside, aching and wanting and needing. When he held her, she wasn't embarrassed or afraid. She simply wanted him, wanted this man she cared for more than she should.

It was already too late to protect her heart, she realized. She was falling, falling hard, and there was nothing she could do, short of leaving now. Leaving, going to the airport, climbing on a plane, and flying back to New York, where she would get another job and never, ever see Renzo again.

She should run away now, but she didn't have the strength.

"I don't understand this," she said, her voice full of anguish. "Because you shouldn't, shouldn't…"

He gripped her shoulders and forced her to look at him. "Stop trying to tell me what I should and shouldn't want." He took her hand, dragged it down his torso, to the evidence of his desire for her. Already, he was hard again, and she gasped as she wrapped her hand around him.

His breath hitched in, and her bones dissolved. How could she walk away from this?

She couldn't. It was impossible. And he knew it, too.

He pressed her back on the bed, turning her until she was on her knees. And then he showed her another way to tumble headlong into pleasure, entering her from behind so that she gasped at the erotic fullness of his possession. His fingers skimmed over the sensitive heart of her even as he moved so exquisitely inside her. When she flew apart this time, he gave her no quarter, gripping her hips and thrusting into her until he came with a ragged cry and they collapsed together onto the bed.

Then he pulled her into the curve of his body and anchored her to him with a hand firmly on her hip. Once more she tumbled, only this time it was into the sweet oblivion of sleep.

CHAPTER ELEVEN

THERE was a rumbling in Faith's ear. Someone was mowing grass and the sound of the mower was filtering into her consciousness, waking her slowly. But, no, the sound was warmer than a mower. And then a cold, wet nose tickled her ear and Faith's eyes snapped open.

Lola lay curled on the pillow next to her, purring happily. Faith turned her head. Renzo was standing near the window, naked except for the towel wrapped around his waist, coffee cup in one hand, other hand propped against the window frame above his head.

He turned when she stirred. And then he moved toward the bed and her heart squeezed so tight she couldn't get her next breath out. Lola lifted her head and mewed, then bounded toward Renzo as he perched on the side of the bed. He laughed and scooped her up, nuzzling his cheek against her fur before putting her down again.

Faith's heart thumped hard. The thin ice beneath her cracked just a little more, threatening her with a headlong plunge into emotions she wasn't prepared to deal with just yet.

Renzo looked up at her, his eyes clouding over. "What is wrong, Faith? Did I hurt you last night?"

Yes. Because it was beautiful and magical—and it wouldn't last. He wasn't hers, and she was just another in a long line of women who'd fallen into his bed and under his spell. Even though she'd known better.

"No, of course not," she said, shifting herself higher in the bed until she was sitting back against the pillows.

He didn't look convinced. "I'm sorry if I was…rough," he said. "I should not have taken you like that when this is still so new to you."

Her ears were hot. She couldn't meet his gaze. Lola wandered over and stretched her little paws against Faith's leg. Faith stroked the silky head, her heart so full of feeling for man and beast that she thought she would burst with it.

"There is nothing you did to me that I did not want," she admitted, her gaze firmly fixed on the gray-striped kitten. She was afraid to look at him, not because she was embarrassed, but because she was afraid he would see what was in her heart.

But he wouldn't allow her that kind of evasion. He tilted her chin up with a finger, forced her to look at him. Neither of them said anything for a long moment. Her blood rushed through her veins, swirled in her head and heart until she felt dizzy.

"How do you feel this morning?" he asked.

Like I'm in deep, deep trouble. "Fabulous," she said. "Slightly sore, but not unpleasantly so."

"Regrets?"

"No."

His expression was doubtful, but he didn't say anything. She could tell him that she had no regrets now, but she knew she would eventually—when he left her for someone else and her heart shattered into a million pieces.

She tickled Lola's chin. The kitten swatted at her and she laughed. "I'm glad you went and got her." She pictured him crossing over to her room and scooping Lola from her nest in the bathroom. That he even remembered the tiny kitten made her heart swell.

"She needs you as well as I."

Needs. She told herself not to read anything into that word, but she couldn't help it if it made her feel as though she'd swallowed sunshine.

There was something else she'd been thinking about, too. "Thank you for believing me last night, Renzo. It means a lot."

His blue eyes seemed to see inside to her soul as he sat and watched her. "You don't trust people, do you?"

Lola curled against her leg and Faith rested a hand on the tiny purring body. "I—I'm just cautious."

"Why? Who hurt you, Faith?"

"I don't know what you mean." It was evasion, pure and simple. And it wasn't working, because he was looking at her like he knew better. He *did* know better, she realized. Something about that knowledge pricked her to her core. He could see right through her, and she still knew nothing about him. Other than he had a big heart and a stubborn streak a mile wide.

And that his reputation as a lover wasn't in the least bit exaggerated, she thought with a twinge of heat.

"I think you do," he said softly. "Something happened to you. Something that made you leave home and never want to go back. Something that made you unwilling to trust."

Faith's shoulders sagged beneath the weight of his words. She was tired of being cautious, of carrying her burdens alone. It wasn't tragic, what had happened—though she'd certainly thought so at the time.

No, with the perspective of years and distance, it was simply humiliating. Once she'd left Cottonwood behind, she'd never told anyone. She'd been terrified to tell anyone, as if it would bring the whole ugly business up again.

"Yes," she said softly. "You're right. But it's not what you think. It's just, um, embarrassing."

"As embarrassing as my first sexual experience?" he said, one corner of his mouth turning up in a grin.

Faith smiled. "Worse, actually." She toyed with the edge of the coverlet. "I had a boyfriend I thought I was terribly in love with in high school. It was assumed we would get married once school was over."

"But you did not."

"No." She sighed as she let herself remember the ugly events of her senior year. "His name was Jason, and my parents adored him. He wanted to, uh, go all the way—and I didn't. It almost happened, on my parents couch when they were out one night. But it didn't, and Jason was angry with me.

"He texted me later, telling me it was over between us. Unless I proved I loved him." Faith sucked in a breath, remembering how naive she'd been. How trusting and gullible and downright stupid. "I sent him a picture I took with my phone."

"A picture?"

Faith closed her eyes. Even now, the humiliation was intense. "A naked picture, Renzo. I wasn't smart enough to cut my head out of the picture when I took it. It was clearly me—and Jason sent it to a friend. Who sent it to another friend, and on and on. You get the idea. My parents were furious. I made my father look bad, you see, since he was a minister."

Renzo reached over and squeezed her hand. "This is why you haven't spoken to them in eight years?"

The lump in her throat ached. Her family hadn't stood beside her at all. They'd thrown her to the wolves, and all because of her father's self-righteousness. "Yes. It was hell, absolute hell, going to that school for the rest of the year. Everyone laughed at me. Everyone pointed and talked about me. I lost all my friends. I was mortified."

She took a deep breath, determined to hold her angry tears at bay. It was cathartic to tell someone, and so very hard at the same time. "But my parents wouldn't take me out of school or let me go to another school. They made me keep going until I graduated—which I barely did since I stopped studying and getting good grades. My dad thought it was a fitting punishment for my sins. When I graduated, I left town and I've never looked back. I even changed my last name so I could feel like someone new."

She'd had to change her name because the thought of being Faith Winston made her physically ill. It was so much easier to become someone else, another Faith who had never done something as stupid as send a naked photo to a boy. Reinventing herself had been the only way to survive.

Renzo looked furious, but he leaned back against the headboard and pulled her into the curve of his arm. "You were young," he said fiercely. "You didn't do anything wrong."

"I was stupid," she said. "And because I was eighteen, the authorities did nothing about it. I imagine you could still find the picture if you typed Faith Winston into a search engine."

Renzo swore softly. "I'm sure you were absolutely beautiful, but I have no desire to see this photo when I have the real Faith warm and naked in my bed. And you were not stupid, *cara mia*. You were young. And in love with someone who did not deserve you."

He handed her his cup of coffee. She took it silently, sipped. It was such an intimate gesture, but she was determined not to think it meant more than it did. No doubt he was always this solicitous with his lovers. And, right now, he felt sorry for her.

"Why don't we get dressed and go into Florence?" he said a few moments later. "We'll have lunch there, and I'll take you to see the *David*."

"I'd love that," she said wistfully. "But you have a meeting this afternoon. I remember because I went over your calendar when we returned from the factory."

And as much as she wanted to go to Florence with him, to pretend they were a normal couple on a date, she couldn't let him down when it was her duty to manage his appointments. They might have spent one night together, but she was still his PA. The job came first.

He took the coffee from her and placed it on the bedside table. And then he tilted her head back, kissing her until she squirmed with the sizzling tension coiling inside her body.

"Cancel it," he murmured a few minutes later. "In fact, cancel getting dressed, too. At least for another hour…"

Renzo was on edge in a way he couldn't recall ever feeling before.

He trailed after Faith, who walked through the Accademia Gallery and oohed and ahhed at everything like a child at her first carnival. She was so lovely and sweet that he couldn't imagine the sort of family who would be cruel to her. How could anyone want to hurt Faith?

She strolled along, oblivious to his dark thoughts. She'd temporarily forgotten him, and it made him oddly jealous. He wanted her to look at him the way she was looking at the art, wanted her to turn and slip her arm around his waist and stroll beside him, her warmth pressing into him.

He'd loved the expression on her face when they'd first entered the long Galleria del David where Michelangelo's *Prisoners* lined the walls. Her soft pink mouth had dropped open, her eyes growing wide. She'd studied each of the *Prisoners* before making her way to the David, who stood on his pedestal beneath the dome at one end of the long gallery.

Voices echoed throughout the chamber, but it was also solemn, thanks to the guards stationed nearby who refused to allow shouting or running—or camera flashes. Faith stopped and stood with her head tilted back and her jaw loose as she let her gaze skim the perfect form of the sculpture.

Faith studied the statue, but Renzo studied her. He'd often heard about a woman glowing—when she'd had fabulous sex, when she was in love, when she was pregnant—but he'd never noticed that glow until today.

There was something about her that drew his eye and wouldn't let him look away. She moved with a grace that was far more sensual than he'd realized before. He didn't usually pay attention to women's fashion, other than to note how a woman looked in her clothes, but he'd found himself analyzing Faith's clothing and wishing he could remove it. Not because she looked dowdy or boxy or unattractive, but because she looked chic and put together and it annoyed him when men turned to look at her.

And plenty of them had turned to look at her.

She'd worn a casual dress with sandals. The dress accented her waist, her breasts, and flared over her hips into a swingy skirt that fluttered and swirled when she moved. Her legs were bare, and he found himself thinking of how they'd felt wrapped around his waist as he'd taken her body into sweet oblivion.

She'd been so innocent, and so carnal at the same time. He thought back to the moment he'd unwrapped her like a present, and his body grew as hard as the Carrara marble on the pedestal.

"It's wonderful," she said, turning to him and reaching for his hand, her eyes shining with unshed tears that caused his chest to ache.

"*Si*, it is quite magnificent."

"Thank you for bringing me."

He tugged her into the circle of his arms, uncaring that others moved around them like water flowing around a rock in the stream. "I can think of a few ways you can show your appreciation later," he told her.

Her eyes widened as she felt the strength of his desire for her. "How can you possibly be…?"

He grinned at the word she did not say. *Aroused. Ready?* "Aren't you?"

The heat of a blush spread over her cheeks. "Yes, I have to confess that I am." She put her forehead against his chest. "I can't believe you've managed to turn me into the kind of woman who would rather spend the day in bed with you than do just about anything else."

He threaded his fingers into the silk of her hair. "I would have been happy to oblige had I known."

She looked up at him again. "If I weren't starving, I'd suggest we leave right now and go back to the villa."

Possessiveness, hot and sharp, flared inside him. "Ah, but there is no need, *cara*. I have an apartment nearby. But first, lunch."

He took her hand and led her from the gallery. They emerged onto the street and walked a few blocks to one of his favorite Florentine restaurants. They were greeted like old friends and shown to a table on the terrace with a lovely view of the Duomo. Usually, Renzo liked a bit more privacy, but since it was Faith's first time in Italy, he wanted to indulge her appetite for adventure.

They started with a beef Carpaccio that was so thin and tender it melted in the mouth, a *mozzarella di bufala* and tomato salad, and then moved on to a luscious spaghetti carbonara before finishing with *panna cotta* and espresso. Faith ate everything with gusto, her eyes closing from time to time while she sighed and licked her lips.

It was refreshing to see a woman eat something other than a salad for a change. American women—especially the ones like Katie Palmer and Lissa Stein—seemed to subsist on nothing but lettuce and water for the most part.

But then he had to acknowledge that it was more the *sort* of woman he'd dated rather than a cultural trait. The Faith Blacks of the world seemed to have no trouble enjoying a good meal. Faith was so refreshing, so different—so real. Why had he avoided real women in his life? Why had he always chosen the ones who, deep down, repelled him?

In spite of his desire to get Faith alone again, he was also enjoying her company. They lingered over their coffee, talking about things like how he got started building motorcycles, what had made him want to race and how she'd ended up in New York. For the first time ever, he found himself wanting to share more about himself with her than he had with anyone else.

Faith knew what it was like to be ostracized from her family. Knew how it felt to have a father care more for himself and his reputation than he did for you. She would understand—and yet he couldn't quite bring himself to tell her. He wasn't golden like Niccolo Gavretti, who came from a supremely wealthy family with pedigree and influence, and who'd grown up with every privilege.

He was a mongrel in comparison, a cur slipping into back alleys and stealing food and clothing. He couldn't tell Faith that, couldn't bear the pity or the disgust in her eyes if he did.

So he said nothing.

The sun dipped lower in the sky and golden light bathed the square, turning everything he'd always taken for granted into something magical. Or perhaps that was because he was seeing it through her eyes.

Nothing that good could last, however. Soon, he began to notice camera flashes. At first, he thought it was tourists—but then the flashes became more numerous, and directed toward them. Renzo swore, and Faith turned to look, her expression falling after the picture snapped.

He knew what she was afraid of, and he wanted to leap over the railing and rip the cameras away from the paparazzi. He wanted to smash them into a million pieces and protect her from any fear of her old photo coming to light again.

But an action like that would only inflame their curiosity, so instead he took her hand and tugged her toward the back of the restaurant. He laid a handful of bills on the counter for the owner, who apologized profusely, and then they exited the restaurant into the alley behind it and hurried toward another alley.

Renzo took her on a crisscross trip through the city, but the photographers never caught up to them. Soon, he slowed their pace until they were strolling pleasantly along as if everything was normal.

"I'm sorry, Faith. I had hoped that wouldn't happen."

"You're a public person. It was inevitable." She seemed troubled and he stopped, turned to face her. She didn't look at him at first, but when she did, he could see the worry in her eyes.

His heart squeezed at the look on her face. He knew how much that impulsive nude photo had affected her, how much it had shaped her life. It would have been hell to endure what she'd endured. "You are concerned that if you appear in the paper with me, someone will find that old picture of you, aren't you?"

She shrugged, and he knew she was trying to put a brave

face on it. "It's silly. I'm no one. Who's going to care about an old nude photo that isn't even all that good? It would take an extraordinary effort to find it, and then to connect it to the woman I am today."

Yet with the press, anything was possible. Especially where it concerned his life. They'd dug up just about everything he'd ever done. The only thing they didn't know was who his father was. He didn't protect the *conte*'s identity for the man's family—or even for his own, since the *conte* no longer had the power to harm them—but because he didn't want the old man to have any credit for who Renzo had become.

"I wish I could tell you it won't happen, but the truth is that I don't know." He put his hands on her shoulders and bent until he was looking her in the eye. "I promise you that I will do everything in my power to find and destroy that photo before it can happen."

She shook her head. "It's out there, Renzo. I don't think even you can make it go away for good." She sighed. "I knew if I were seen with you, there was a good chance I'd end up in the papers. And I was willing to take the risk. So whatever happens next, I'll deal with it."

She looked determined, strong, even though he knew she was afraid. But that was Faith: practical and brave, and convinced she had to look after herself because no one else would. He pulled her into his arms and hugged her tight. "*We* will deal with it, *cara*, should it come to pass."

"It's sure to thrill Cottonwood if it gets that far," she grumbled. "I think I was the most excitement they'd had since Sherman marched to the sea and burned the town down around their ears."

Renzo blinked. Her voice was syrupy and sweet with that slow drawl he loved, but he didn't understand the reference. "What is Sherman?"

She laughed softly. "A Civil war general typically reviled in the South. It happened over one hundred years ago. It was very exciting, according to Miss Minnie Blaine, who's nearly one hundred herself and remembers her grandmama talking about it when she was a child."

"I should like to visit this South someday," he said truthfully. "It sounds fascinating."

She pushed back and arched an eyebrow. "I can see you there, Renzo. Eating barbecued ribs and drinking sweet tea. You'd be the third most exciting thing to happen to Cottonwood."

"Only the third?" he teased. "Perhaps I should do something a bit more scandalous first."

She laughed. "Perhaps you'd care to text a nude photo of yourself to the town elders? That would surely get some blood pumping."

"Happily, *cara*, if it meant they would forget about your photo."

She looked wistful, and he reached out to push a strand of hair from her face. "They will never forget it. I am persona non grata in Cottonwood."

"I doubt that," he said. "But I understand why you think so. It was a long time ago, and you are a very successful career woman now. Would they truly not welcome you back if you wanted to go?"

She frowned. "I don't want to go. Ever."

He understood her conviction. They were more alike than she knew, but instead of telling her so he took her hand and pressed it to his lips. Then they continued down the street, threading their way back toward the apartment and talking about the differences between Georgia and Italy. He was so lost in the conversation that he didn't realize where they were until it was too late. They emerged from a narrow alley between buildings, out onto a wider thoroughfare, and he realized his mistake. He'd come here as if on autopilot, and he stiffened even as Faith gasped at the magnificent villa before them.

"Oh, it's gorgeous," she exclaimed. "Does someone actually live there, or is it open to tourists?"

The wrought iron fence surrounding the Villa de Lucano was imposing, but the house that sat back from the street was ornate, part of its facade carved from Carrara marble and carefully timeworn in that way that only houses in the Old World could be.

The gardens were vast, lush, manicured. A fountain gurgled somewhere out of sight. Renzo imagined children playing there, imagined a father coming outside to greet them after time away, bending to hug them all as they flew into his open arms. It was an old fantasy, and not a particularly welcome one.

"No, it is a private residence," he said, unable to hide the bitterness in his voice.

She turned to him, her soft eyes questioning. And, in spite of everything she'd shared with him, he still couldn't seem tell her the shameful truth of his life before he'd become Lorenzo D'Angeli, tycoon, Grand Prix bad boy, superstar.

He wasn't ready for that. Didn't know if he would ever be ready for it. He would never, ever allow his life to sink to that level again. Anger surged through him.

He had to win the championship. *Had to.*

Success was everything. Renzo wanted his father to choke on his success, to regret every single day that he had not found a way to be a part of his son's life. The *conte* was proud, and Renzo was the richest, the most successful of his children. And no one knew.

"Is everything okay, Renzo? Does your leg hurt?"

"A bit," he said, seizing on the excuse. His leg did hurt, but it was a mild discomfort more than anything.

She looked contrite, and for that he felt a pinprick of guilt. He knew she blamed herself, as if the walking was her fault.

"It's not far now," he said, guiding her away from the Villa de Lucano. "Just a few minutes more."

Once they reached the apartment, Renzo laid his keys on a table and went to look out the huge plate window fronting the living area. He'd picked this apartment because of the city view, and because it was the best money could buy. He could see the rooftop of the Villa de Lucano, but that didn't usually bother him.

Now, however, it irritated him.

He stood with his hands in his pockets and stared at nothing in particular. Faith came to his side and quietly studied the view with him.

"What is it, Renzo?" she finally said when he didn't move or speak. "I know something is bothering you, and I know it's not your leg."

He closed his eyes for a moment. Of course she knew. She was attuned to him somehow. He didn't understand the connection between them, but he knew there was one. It was odd, and yet somehow necessary, too.

The words he didn't want to say burned at the back of his throat until he had to let them out or choke on them. "It's that place. The Villa de Lucano."

She pulled him around to face her, her green eyes wide and full of concern. "What is it about that place that bothers you so much?"

He studied her for the longest time—the sheen of moisture in her eyes, the determined set to her jaw, the high color in her cheeks. She'd endured much humiliation, and she'd survived it. She'd reinvented herself, the same as he had. She understood what it took to do so.

"The Conte de Lucano is my father," he found himself saying. And once he'd said that much, he told her the rest. What did it matter? "He does not want to know me. He never has."

He watched the emotions play over her face: confusion, anger, sadness and worry.

"Oh Renzo, I'm sorry," she finally said, her voice barely more than a whisper. A moment later, a single tear spilled down her cheek. It stunned him that she would cry for him. He caught the droplet with his thumb, smoothed it away.

"Tears, *cara*?" he asked.

She closed her eyes and shook her head, as if shaking the tears away. "I'm just emotional. It's part of being a girl."

He laughed in spite of himself. In spite of the vise squeezing his chest. She made him laugh, even when he did not want to. He pulled her closer and dipped to nuzzle her hair. He ached inside, but for once it was almost bearable.

"I like very much that you're a girl."

And then, because he didn't want to talk anymore—because he didn't think he *could* talk anymore—he swept her off her feet and carried her into the bedroom.

CHAPTER TWELVE

FAITH looked up from her computer, her heart doing that funny little flip thing it always did as the door to Renzo's office opened. They were spending days at the factory now while he went over the details for the Viper and for the next production launch. The launch was timed to coincide with the Viper's debut on the Grand Prix circuit, and everyone was working long hours to make it happen smoothly.

She'd never been so happy and so miserable at the same time. She was happy because she enjoyed being Renzo's lover, and miserable because she felt as if she'd done everything wrong. The other office staff kept their distance. She knew why. It wasn't a language barrier, as everyone spoke English, but more of a perception barrier. She was the boss's girlfriend, and everyone knew it.

It was, in some respects, a nightmare. She felt their censure, and it felt far too much like the censure she'd gotten at home when the photo of her began to circulate. People were distant, judgmental. They whispered behind her back.

She hated the way it made her feel. As if she were different. Damaged.

It had been inevitable, she supposed. The pictures of the two of them had finally appeared in the paper after the night in Florence when they'd been photographed together at the restaurant. Those photos were innocuous, but when you added in the photo of the kiss at the party, it didn't take a genius to put two and two together.

Her heart had beat so hard when she'd seen that picture that she'd thought she would pass out. Renzo had hugged her to him and told her not to worry. So far, he'd been right. There'd been nothing about her real name or the photograph that had caused her so much pain.

Still, she feared the feelings it would dredge up once the photo was public knowledge again. She'd thought she could handle it, but now, with the office staff treating her like she was a leper, she wasn't quite so confident.

She smiled as Renzo approached. He was as mind-numbingly delicious as always as he came over to her desk, clad in a custom suit and loafers, his dark hair curling over his collar. His blue eyes were sharp, but she could see the strain in them. He'd been pushing himself relentlessly, riding the Viper, working on the details for the launch—and making love to her at night in his bed.

A tendril of heat coiled in her belly and her body responded with a surge. Those nights were the hottest, most incredible she'd ever known. Renzo had taught her things she'd have blushed at only a few weeks ago, but things that she now did hungrily, greedily, as if she couldn't get enough of him.

Which, she acknowledged, she couldn't.

But she wanted more than just the physical from him. She wanted his heart, his trust. She'd thought perhaps she was starting to get those things that night in Florence when he'd told her who his father was, but they'd not spoken of it since. They'd spoken of nothing so deeply emotional again. It was as if he regretted letting her see inside his life.

"Did that fax from Robert Stein arrive?" he asked.

"It just came through," she replied, handing him the papers she'd taken from the machine only a moment before he'd opened the door.

He took it, frowning as he looked it over, and her heart squeezed tight with all the emotions she had to keep bottled inside. She felt hot and achy and needy every time she looked at him.

But it was more than that.

Whenever he touched her, whenever he played with Lola, everything inside her hurt. In a good way. She knew what it was, even if she'd never felt quite this way before. She was in love with him, but she didn't dare tell him.

He'd shown absolutely no signs of returning her feelings, and she wasn't about to commit the mistake that she was certain other women had committed in the past.

And yet it made her angry, too. Why couldn't she be herself? Why couldn't she speak up and tell him how she felt? Why was she afraid to do so? If he threw her out, then at least she would know where she stood, wouldn't she? Why waste time loving someone who didn't love you back?

There was another side to her despair, as well. Every time Renzo went onto the track, she could hardly breathe. He'd been training hard, riding the Viper and icing his leg at night. She'd tried to convince him to see a doctor, to hire a masseuse, but he was stubborn and wouldn't do it.

So she massaged his leg, praying that it was enough, that today would not be the day his leg would cramp up at two hundred miles an hour. She could stand it when he was alone on the track—but when he entered the circuit, and there were other screaming motorcycles all around him?

How could he stop if something happened? How could he possibly get out of the way in time?

He looked up then and caught her watching him. The answering heat in his eyes sent a surge of relief rushing through her. For now, at least, he was hers.

He glanced toward the open hallway that led to his suite of offices. No one was in sight, so he bent and fitted his lips to hers. She knew she should push him away, but she couldn't do it. It had been hours since she'd kissed him.

He smelled delicious, and so very sinful. She wanted to strip away his clothes and lick her way down his body. And then she wanted to take him in her mouth and feel the power she had over him as he gasped and groaned his pleasure.

"Come into the office with me," he said. "We'll lock the door and—"

She put a hand over his mouth to silence him. "You know I can't do that. Your people already dislike me enough. Especially that secretary you shuffled to another office."

He darted his tongue out to lick her palm, then straightened again. "No one dislikes you, *cara mia*. And it was time for Signora Leoni to go. She never kept my appointments straight. But if you feel people don't like you, you can work from home."

Home. It was his home, not hers, but she loved it anyway. She was happy there, and not because it was beautiful and far more lush than she was accustomed to in her life, but because Renzo was there. And Lola, her sweet little kitten who was growing in leaps and bounds. Lola owned the place now. Even stodgy Fabrizio couldn't resist her kitten antics.

Faith lowered her lashes. "I think you underestimate the benevolence of your staff, Renzo. They dislike me because they know we're together. But I won't leave. I'll be fine working here."

His hand ghosted over her hair. "You never give up, do you, Faith?"

She met his curious gaze. "I believe in working hard

to get what I want. And I'm not going to let what anyone else thinks stop me."

He bent and kissed her swiftly. "This is why I like you so much," he said. "We are exactly alike, *cara*."

Like? Her mind focused on that one word and wouldn't let it go. Like. He liked her. After everything they'd shared, he *liked* her.

It stung. She turned back to her computer, angry that sudden tears pricked the backs of her eyes. Well, honestly, what had she expected? She'd known she shouldn't get involved with him, but she'd gone down that road with very little hesitation when it came right to it.

"Have I said something?" he asked from behind her.

She shook her head. "Of course not. But I have a lot of correspondence to get through before the day is over. And you have a conference call in half an hour."

"Ah, *si*, I do." He sounded tired, and she turned to look at him. He ran the fingers of one hand through his hair.

Worry pricked her. "You need to rest, Renzo. Nothing good will come of it if you keep burning the candle at both ends."

Fatigue lines bracketed his mouth and eyes. "It is always this way before the season starts."

"I can't imagine it's good for you when you need your strength."

"There are a lot of things that aren't good for me. But they must be done."

"But your leg—"

"I'm fine, *cara*," he snapped suddenly.

Faith gaped at him. It was as if she'd reached out to pet sweet little Lola and been bitten for her trouble. His expression was a mix of rage, bitterness and despair. She knew that he was tired, that he was worried, and that he was angry over the hand fate had dealt him.

But he would not share any of it with her. He would not tell her how he felt, or how scared he was. It hurt. After all she thought they'd shared together, he would not open up to her now. Instead, he lashed out, pushed her away.

She was no different to him than Katie Palmer. And that made her angry.

"I think we both know better," she said, her heart throbbing. "You might deny it to everyone else, but you aren't denying it to me."

His jaw worked, his eyes flashing with a different kind of heat than they had a moment ago. "Type your letters, Faith," he said. And then he turned and walked back into his office, shutting the door firmly behind him. Shutting her out.

Renzo went back to his desk and collapsed in the chair. He felt like an ass for snapping at Faith. But he'd been feeling edgier than ever lately. He was tired, and his leg throbbed almost nonstop these days. The pain was bearable, but only just.

Yet he knew if he told her the truth, she'd beg him not to ride the Viper. And he simply did not want to have that conversation with her.

With anyone.

Since the night a little over a week ago when they'd stumbled onto the *via* opposite the Villa de Lucano, he'd been more determined than ever to make the Viper a success. And the only way that was happening was if he kept the reins for a little while longer. His team was good, but a victory didn't mean as much to them as it did to him.

He'd thought about pulling out. He really had. But the media expected him to ride. His investors expected him to do so, as well. The whole world was waiting for Renzo D'Angeli, the Iron Prince, to zoom onto the track and claim the ultimate victory for the tenth time. It would be a great feat, and everyone was watching.

Some were hoping he would fail. Niccolo Gavretti, of course. And quite possibly his father. They had never spoken, but Renzo knew his father followed the sport. He'd even seen the *conte* in the paddock once before. Backing Gavretti, naturally. The De Lucanos and the Gavrettis were old friends, blue bloods who stuck together in business and in life.

Renzo tossed down the papers that he'd been trying to concentrate on and leaned back in his chair, propping his leg on a low table that he'd pulled over for the purpose.

Dio. He rubbed the knotted muscles hard, hoping to ease the pain. He thought of calling Faith, but she was angry with him. Besides, he didn't want to admit that she'd been right. He couldn't admit it.

He slipped open a desk drawer and pulled out a bottle of over-the-counter painkillers. He shook two pills into his hand—and then shook out two more. He had to remain focused on the goal. Everything else was secondary.

He took the pills, and then picked up the phone and punched in a number. When a familiar voice answered on the third ring, he knew he was doing the right thing. For her, he would win again. For her, he would rub victory in the *conte*'s face once more.

"Renzo," his mother said. "*Ciao,* darling!"

They were at the factory late. Renzo rode the Viper again, zooming around the track at speeds Faith was certain were somehow faster than he'd ever ridden before. When he dismounted, there was no hitch in his gate, no weakness that she could detect. He'd had a great few days, though she knew it was only a matter of time before the pain got to be too much for him.

He kept a bottle of painkillers on the nightstand, rationing them out as if they were the last, most precious pills on earth. She admired his strength of will even while she cursed his stubbornness. If he would take them more regularly, or see a doctor, perhaps something could be done. Something that would ensure his safety on the track.

After he showered and dressed, they drove into Florence where they went to his apartment and changed for the evening. There was another party tonight, another gathering of investors and people who followed the MotoGP circuit. The season would start soon and all the teams would be heading to Qatar for the first race.

Eighteen races in thirteen countries. It was a grueling circuit, with two or three races each month, plus all the travel that was required to move from country to country. The logistics of it were a nightmare. Now that she knew what Renzo actually did, it was no wonder she'd worked at D'Angeli's New York factory for months before she'd ever seen him in person.

She loved being here with him, but she almost wished she'd remained in the financial office of the company. If she had, she wouldn't be so desperately in love with him now. She wouldn't be here, praying that every time he took that beast of a motorcycle on the track, he'd make it out alive.

Faith looked at the dress she'd selected for tonight and felt her heart thump hard. It was more daring than anything she'd yet worn. Black, made of clingy jersey, and figure hugging from the strapless bosom to her ankles. There was a slit up one side that went as high as midthigh.

She finished her hair and slipped into the dress, then slid her feet into glittery peep-toe platforms. She studied her appearance in the mirror, pleased with the elegant sensuality portrayed before her. Yes, it was a long way from the preacher's daughter to this, but she was comfortable, confident in the way she looked.

When she joined Renzo in the foyer, his gaze glided over her approvingly. But then his expression clouded.

"I'm not sure I want you going out like that, *cara*." He kissed her on the cheek and she inhaled his clean, fresh scent, closing her eyes for a brief second as she did so. "You look...too sexy for your own good."

Faith reached for her wrap, her pulse thrumming. "Nevertheless, it's what I'm wearing. I brought nothing else with me."

She hadn't forgotten that he'd dismissed her earlier, though it seemed as if he had. She thought for a minute he might pull her close and kiss her properly, but she was glad he did not. She couldn't quite bear it right now, when she was fighting with herself over what she meant to his life.

They arrived at the party, held at one of Florence's museums, fashionably late. Reporters and photographers were stationed outside the exclusive location, snapping pics and shouting questions to everyone who arrived. Faith hesitated before exiting the car. Renzo squeezed her hand, and she found the strength to join him on the red carpet. She always felt as if she didn't belong, and yet while he held on to her, she could do anything.

Faith pasted a smile on her face as they moved down the line. Renzo stopped every so often, smiling for the cameras as he anchored her to his side like a pretty ornament.

Finally, they passed inside. The host and hostess greeted them, fawning over Renzo before he extracted himself from their grip. The next guest came in, and the routine started all over again.

Faith accepted a glass of champagne from a waiter passing by with a tray. Between the paparazzi just now and Renzo's reaction to her concerns earlier, her nerves were frayed tonight. She sipped the liquid, hoping it would at least take the edge off.

She couldn't stop thinking about the way Renzo had shut down when she'd mentioned his leg. It bothered her a great deal that he would cut her from the important parts of his life, that he would refuse to discuss something so elemental as his fitness to do the job he intended to do. Was she just supposed to accept his edict and hope for the best?

Yes, clearly, she was. Faith tried not to frown as they moved through the gathering. Renzo introduced her to so many people she would never remember them all. She noted that while he did not say she was his PA, he also did not say she was his girlfriend. He introduced her simply as Faith.

It was a silly thing to focus on, but it was yet one more piece of evidence piled onto all the rest that had her wondering about her place in his life. Was this how it began for the other women he'd been with? Did they all start searching for signs that they meant more to him than just a warm body in his bed?

You knew, she told herself. *You knew what this was, and you did it anyway.*

She didn't say much, but then she wasn't expected to. Renzo stayed by her side for the longest time, but then he got caught in a crowd of men who wanted to talk motorcycles and ended up drifting away from her. In a way, she was relieved. She wasn't in the mood for a party, and it meant she could escape somewhere quiet for a few moments.

Faith glided through the rooms of the museum, studying the art, enjoying the rarity of having a gallery to herself while she was dressed up and sipping champagne. This certainly wasn't the kind of life she'd led before becoming Renzo's lover, and it would not be the kind she led after. If her old friends in Cottonwood could see her now, wouldn't they be surprised?

"Abandoned, *bella*?"

Faith gasped at the voice as she spun to find Niccolo Gavretti watching her from the entrance. He looked sinful in his tuxedo and white shirt, but he did not move her. For a moment, she wished he did. How easy would it be if she could just cast off her current lover for a new one?

"I am not abandoned," she said coolly. "Renzo is busy."

"I noticed," he said, his lips curving in a smile. "And he will only get busier once the season starts. There will be no time at all for lovely distractions when he is so focused on winning."

Ice dripped down her spine as she gripped the glass hard and tried not to react. "I'm sure I'll survive," she said.

He smiled his cool predator's smile. "I am sure you will, *bella*."

He crossed the room to her side, tilted his head back to study the painting of a weeping Madonna. It was a beautiful picture, dark and lovely, with the most vibrant blues and golds that made Mary stand out from the rest of the scene.

"If you wish for a change, lovely Faith, I am certain we could have a good time together. I promise I would not leave you to amuse yourself while I caroused with my buddies." His silvery eyes fixed on her and she shivered. There was nothing but coldness behind that gaze. Ruthlessness.

Another time, before she'd fallen in love with Renzo, she might have been flattered. But she knew Niccolo's goal in approaching her now that she'd been caught between them once before. He only wanted to annoy Renzo. It had nothing at all to do with her.

And she wasn't tempted anyway. Far from it.

"I don't like change," she said, her voice a touch sharp. "If you will excuse me."

He laughed. "You have only to let me know if you change your mind."

"I won't."

Her pulse raced as she brushed past him, but he didn't try to stop her. She headed for the noise of the more-populated areas of the museum. As soon as she stepped out of the gallery, she ran into Renzo. Her heart thumped.

He was frowning. "I've been looking for you, *cara mia.*"

"And now you've found me," she said brightly. Too brightly, because his gaze sharpened. Damn Niccolo Gavretti.

"What have you been doing all alone, Faith?"

"Looking at paintings," she said. "They are really quite amazing."

She heard footsteps behind her, and knew precisely who it was. Knew what Renzo would see and what he would think. And she suddenly didn't feel like pretending anymore. She'd done nothing wrong, and if he couldn't trust that she hadn't, then she wanted to know it.

"*Ciao,* Renzo."

He stiffened. She could see his entire body go rigid, his eyes flashing fire. "Nico," he replied, his voice cold in spite of the angry heat in his gaze.

"I'm looking forward to our match in Qatar."

Renzo vibrated with anger. "I'm not sure why. The Viper is far better than anything you've designed lately—assuming you haven't stolen anything that does not belong to you."

Niccolo's eyes flashed. "Still banging that drum, Renzo?"

"We both know the motorcycles are not your true passion. It's simply another way to spend your father's money and stay out of the way doing it, *si?* You could not design an original bike if your life depended upon it."

Niccolo smiled, but it was a flat, lethal curving of the lips that didn't quite reach his eyes. "Arrogant as always, Renzo. I'll enjoy watching you fail."

Renzo's jaw could have been carved from granite. "I won't fail."

"You might." Niccolo strolled toward them, his hands thrust casually into his pockets. Then he stopped and let his gaze slide to Renzo's thigh. "If your leg continues to give you trouble, who knows what will happen?"

CHAPTER THIRTEEN

THEY left the party soon after and returned to Renzo's apartment. Renzo did not speak during the short car ride, and Faith didn't quite know what to say. She wanted to defend herself, to say that she hadn't told Niccolo Gavretti anything, but she couldn't speak. Every time the words formed on her tongue, they wouldn't come out.

Because if she spoke, if she denied it, she sounded guilty. She looked guilty, considering that she'd been alone with the man he hated—the man he'd accused of stealing from him—and she was the only one who knew he'd been having trouble. Except, clearly, she was *not* the only one. Someone else knew, or had at least guessed.

She wanted Renzo to trust her, to believe that she wouldn't tell anyone his secrets.

And yet he was silent.

She waited for him to say something, to ask her to explain, until she couldn't wait anymore. Until they climbed from the car and stood in the darkened street with the cool Tuscan air making her shiver and pull her wrap tighter.

"I didn't tell him, Renzo."

He looked at her over the roof of the sports car. "I did not say you did."

But he sounded cold.

Her heart burned and she felt hot, in spite of the chill. "No, you didn't say anything."

His gaze pinned her, and she knew that he was fighting with himself, that he did in fact think she might have betrayed him.

It hurt more than she'd ever realized it could. How could he possibly think such a thing of her?

They climbed the stairs to his apartment and went inside. Faith removed her wrap and draped it over a chair. Then she kicked her heels off and waited.

"Niccolo Gavretti is not to be trusted, Faith," he finally said. "He will do anything to win, including cheat. He will tell any lie, use any grain of information. You should not talk to him. Ever."

Her stomach twisted. There was certainly more to the story than he'd ever told her before. And if he was going to accuse her of betraying him, then she felt she deserved to know. "What happened between you?"

She wasn't sure he would speak. She watched a hint of sadness chase across his features. But then it was gone, and in its place was the usual fury she saw whenever he spoke of Niccolo.

"We were friends once. Long ago. He knew what my dreams were, what I was planning to do with my designs. Instead of backing me as he promised, he started his own business—with designs remarkably similar to mine."

"He stole from you." It made her sick, and angry. She wanted to punch Niccolo Gavretti's handsome face herself.

"He would love nothing better than to destroy me. I think it would soothe his guilty conscience to know he'd won in the end. Which is why you should not talk to him."

She touched his arm. "I didn't tell him anything, Renzo. Anyone who saw you that first day on the track could have surmised what was happening. You fell to your knees. A lot of people saw it."

His expression grew hard. "You accuse one of my people of spying on me?"

Pain squeezed her belly tight. "Why not? Or am I the only suspect?"

He shoved a hand through his hair and swore. Then he ripped off his bow tie and shrugged out of the bespoke tuxedo jacket. "I know you wouldn't say anything deliberately, Faith. Nico is quite good at extracting what he wants to know."

If he'd stabbed her in the heart with a rusty knife, he couldn't have hurt her more. "I'm not an idiot, Renzo! I didn't say anything to anyone. Ever. Not even accidentally!"

"You could have implied—"

"I implied nothing," she shouted. Fury held her in its cold grip. How could he think she would betray him, even unintentionally? She wouldn't, not ever. Her body shook with the adrenaline pulsing through it.

Renzo stared at her for a long moment. She didn't know what he would do, what he would say—but then he came over and gathered her to him. She stood stiffly in his embrace and refused to soften even while she swallowed angry tears.

"I'm sorry," he said, his lips against her hair. "I'm sorry. I know you would not have said anything."

She put her arms around him and buried her face in his chest. She loved him so much it hurt. And she feared for him.

"I didn't tell him—but maybe you should consider that he's right. You don't know what's going to happen when you get out there."

"It's always been that way on the track, Faith. You never know what will happen. It's part of the challenge."

She clutched his shirt. She was afraid for him, especially now that she knew how much Niccolo Gavretti hated him. "But it's too dangerous now. Maybe you should retire from the circuit. Let someone else do this."

She felt him stiffen and knew she'd said the wrong thing. He pushed her back, holding her at arm's length, and glared at her.

"I'm not retiring, *cara*. Not until I've won."

Her vision was growing blurry, but she no longer cared if she cried or not. "Why do you have to be so stubborn? It's your *life* we're talking about. How many times do you need to win before you'll be satisfied? How many times do you need to prove yourself?"

He turned and went over to the liquor cabinet, poured brandy into a glass. Then he set it down without drinking it, put both his hands on the cabinet, and stood with his back to her for a long moment.

Faith wrapped her arms around herself. She'd gone so far now, way over the line maybe, but for the first time since she'd started to fall for him, she felt as if she'd done the right thing. As if she'd been herself instead of who she thought he wanted her to be. It felt good—and frightening at the same time.

"One more time, Faith," he said. He turned and faced her, his eyes glittering hot. "I need to win one more time."

She sniffled. "Is that one more race or one more championship?"

"You know what it is."

She did. He meant he wanted to win another championship. Eighteen grueling races against a field of competitors who might be just as determined as he was. And who were certainly healthier.

"I'm not sure I can take it," she said softly, truthfully. How could she sit in those stands and watch him each time, her heart in her throat while she waited for something to go wrong?

"I've crashed before. I'll probably crash again. It's part of the sport, *cara*." He picked up the brandy and took a sip. "The goal is not to crash badly. To get up and walk away."

She bit her trembling lip. "And just how are you supposed to do that when you can't even walk without pain most of the time?"

His head snapped up, his nostrils flaring. "I'm fine, Faith. My leg only hurts when the muscles knot. Which is *not* most of the time."

Faith swore. "That's a lie, Renzo, and you know it. I massage it nightly for you. You practically live with an ice pack in the evenings. You're hurting and you're too stubborn to admit you have a problem. You might lie to everyone else, but don't lie to me."

"You go too far," he bit out.

"Do I? I sometimes think I don't go far enough!"

"That's enough, Miss Black," he snapped.

She recoiled as if he'd hit her. And then she gathered herself up, stood straight and tall and glared at him. She knew where she stood with him. Where she would always stand.

"You told me that I didn't trust people, and you were right. But you're a hypocrite, you know that? You don't trust anyone, either. You refuse to let anyone get close to you. You keep everyone at a distance. You cycle through relationships like you cycle through racing leathers. I knew it," she said angrily. "And I was still dumb enough to fall for you."

"We are lovers, not soul mates," he said coolly. "If you expected this from me, I am sorry."

"You aren't," she snapped. "You're only sorry you didn't get the chance to throw me out before I walked away."

He took a step toward her, stopped. Faith's heart was breaking. She'd gone much further over the edge than she'd intended, but it was too late to stop now.

"We'll go to bed," he told her. "Sleep. Tomorrow, everything will look different."

She shook her head. "It won't. Nothing will change the facts. You are injured and you won't admit it, and you intend to kill yourself on the track. I can't stand by and watch you, Renzo. I won't."

"Are you threatening to quit, Faith?"

She snorted. "Quit? Is that how you see this? That I'm quitting my job?"

His jaw tightened. "You can't abandon me right before the season starts. I need you."

Those three words punctured her heart. He didn't need her. He only needed the efficient PA by his side, nothing more. They'd had sex and he'd enjoyed her, but he didn't love her. And he never would.

"My God, my stupidity never ends," she said, half to herself. "I didn't learn my lesson with Jason. I'm just as gullible and needy as I was then. And I want to believe that the man asking me to give him a piece of myself cares for me when I know he doesn't."

"We're good together," he said. "This doesn't need to end."

She laughed, the sound broken and bitter. "Doesn't it? I won't watch you crash and burn, Renzo. I won't be there waiting for something to happen, waiting for them to haul you away in an ambulance because you're too proud to admit you can't do this any longer." She reached for her wrap, shrugged into it blindly. "I'm done. I can't do this."

She fled toward the door, intending to escape into the

Florentine night, to get as far away as she could, but he caught her before she could, turned her with rough hands.

His face was livid. "You aren't leaving me, Faith. I won't let you leave me."

"Then tell me you'll quit," she begged. "Tell me you'll stop this insanity and let someone else race the Viper."

He let her go abruptly and she shot a hand out to steady herself against the wall.

"I won't play this game with you," he said harshly.

"It's not a game," she cried. "I love you, and I don't want to lose you—" She stopped speaking when she realized what she'd said. What she'd revealed.

Renzo stood there before her, looking so cold and cruel. So removed, as if he'd already detached himself from the situation. Which, of course, he had. He'd had a lot of practice, hadn't he?

"I won't stop, Faith." His eyes glittered hot. "If you truly loved me, you wouldn't ask me to."

She could feel the tears trickling down her cheeks. She'd just told him she loved him, and he didn't say anything. Or, he did say something, but something designed to use that love against her.

She wiped the tears away with the back of her hand. "Jason said the same thing, did you know that? He said that if I loved him, I would do what he wanted me to do."

She hadn't had sex with him because she'd been young and scared, but she'd felt the pressure of those words. Felt them so deeply that she made the stupid decision to take that picture for him. To try and appease him.

She would never allow herself to cave in to that kind of pressure again, no matter the cost.

Renzo looked furious. "You can't compare this to what happened eight years ago. I've never asked you to do anything you didn't want to do. I've never threatened you if you didn't. You've made your own choices."

"And I have to keep making them," she said. "I can't stay and watch you go on that track and worry every time that it will be the last."

He shoved his hands in his pockets. "Think carefully, *cara*. If you are asking me to choose between you and riding the Viper, you will lose."

She shook her head sadly. "Don't you think I already know that?"

CHAPTER FOURTEEN

THEY raced at night in Qatar because it was too hot during the day. Renzo stood in the paddock in full leathers, wearing a baseball cap until it was time to put on the helmet and climb onto the shining red-and-white Viper, and talked with the press. Paddock girls pranced around in tight dresses and heels, carrying big umbrellas, but he barely noticed them even when one or two of them purposely came near and shot him coy smiles.

They were sexy and alluring, but they were not Faith. *Dio*, how he missed her. It had been a week since she'd left him, and he'd been miserable just about every moment since then.

She'd told him she loved him, but she'd lied. If she had truly loved him, she wouldn't have left him. And she wouldn't have given him an ultimatum.

His leg ached today, but it ached every day. She was right that he'd kept that from her, just like he'd kept it from everyone. But he was used to the aching. Aching was nothing. Muscle cramps, on the other hand, were a bit more problematic.

He'd been training hard, working the muscles, and he hadn't had an issue in any of the test runs. He would not have an issue today, either.

Faith did not understand that he had to do this. He appreciated that she'd been concerned for him, but if she'd truly loved him, she would have supported him. She would be here with him instead of back in New York, working for one of the other officers in D'Angeli Motors. She'd said she would leave the company and find another job, but he wouldn't let her do it. He'd sent her back with a glowing recommendation, and had heard that she'd been put to work in one of the senior vice president's offices.

He would see her again someday, when he returned to New York to oversee the U.S. operations, but that day would not be anytime soon. Perhaps she would have found someone else by then, a man who could appreciate her and love her for the remarkable woman she was.

His gut twisted hard at the thought of another man loving her. Loving his Faith. He held up his hand to signal the end of the interview and turned and walked away.

He had to get his head into the game today. He could not keep thinking about Faith, about her silky blond hair and her sexy curves, about the way she smiled at him, and the way she hugged that silly cat and said the most ridiculous things to it.

She'd left Lola behind, and he thought it had probably broken her heart more than leaving him had done. But she'd told him, while she stood there with tears in her eyes and hugged the cat close, that Lola would be happier in Tuscany. She had a big house to run and play in, and people there to take care of her. In New York, she'd live in an apartment and be alone most of the day while Faith worked.

Renzo had promised that Lola would have the best care and that she would always have a home with him. Faith had seemed satisfied by that, though she'd quickly put the cat down and walked away after he'd said it.

Out of his life and into the car that would take her to the airport.

He'd been glad he still had Lola after she was gone. The cat slept with him, curled next to his body like a fuzzy rumbling heater, and he sometimes reached over and stroked her soft fur and thought of Faith lying in bed with him and doing the same thing.

Dio, what was wrong with him? Was he a man? Or was he a toothless beast who'd enjoyed cuddling up to a woman and a cat in the middle of the night?

"And where's the lovely Faith today? I had thought she would be by your side, hovering over you like a mother hen until the start."

Renzo looked up to find Niccolo Gavretti sneering at him.

"Faith is not here," he said shortly. He would always despise this man, but he somehow couldn't find the energy to care much today.

"Ah, I see."

Annoyance slid through him at the other man's tone. "Do you?"

Niccolo shrugged. "We are alike, Renzo. We enjoy women, and when we are finished enjoying them, we move on."

Renzo ground his teeth together. "Faith is not just any woman," he said. "And if you ever touch her, I will destroy you."

Gavretti laughed. "If you've discarded her, Renzo, I can hardly see why you'd care."

Renzo took a step toward him, and then stopped, fists clenched at his sides. Gavretti just smiled a slick smile, eyes gleaming in challenge.

"You aren't worth it, Nico." He pulled in a deep breath that was filled with the scents of motor oil and fumes, heard the roar of the crowd in the stands and the growling whine of engines being tweaked and tuned—and he felt empty.

It didn't fill him with elation the way it once had. His blood wasn't pumping hard in his veins, adrenaline wasn't rushing through his body, and he wasn't eager to climb onto the back of the Viper and roar around the track with a pack of other men who were also determined to win.

His lungs filled again with the scents he loved, but again he felt empty. He didn't care. If he rode the Viper to victory or not, he didn't care. It didn't matter what anyone else thought. It only mattered what he thought. What he felt. He had nine world titles, a thriving company and a woman who loved him.

A woman who loved him.

He cared what Faith thought, he realized. He cared a great deal what she thought. It was a revelation to him, a sudden parting of the clouds so that the sun could shine down fully upon him and show him what a fool he'd been. What an utter idiot he was still being if he didn't go after her and beg her to forgive him.

Renzo spun from Gavretti without another word and stalked toward the exit. He had to get out of here, and he had to find Faith and tell her how he felt before he lost her forever.

Faith was frantic. She'd been flying for hours and now she was rushing through the crowd at the Losail Circuit, trying to get to the paddock before the race started.

She'd had to come. She'd been in New York, working and trying to forget that the first race of the season was about to happen. But she'd realized as she sat at her desk and refreshed her computer for the zillionth time, learning the layout of Losail and studying the course, that she'd made a mistake.

She needed to be with Renzo, no matter what happened. No matter what her fears were, it hadn't been fair to ask him to choose between her and the races. She understood that now, and she needed to tell him.

"Matteo," she screamed when she saw the D'Angeli crew chief. She was almost there, but hands were barring her way, stopping her from reaching the D'Angeli team. She'd gotten this far because she still had the cell phone numbers of some of Renzo's team on her phone. She'd called Matteo from the airport in Doha, praying it wasn't too late. He'd promised to get her through to the staging area.

The noise was deafening. The crowd was screaming, the motorcycles were being tuned, and the paddock teemed with reporters and women in tight dresses who paraded around and smiled for the cameras.

"Matteo," she screamed again—and miraculously, his head popped up, his eyes meeting hers across the distance separating them. He spoke to someone, who came rushing over to extract her from the people holding her back. After a hurried conversation over her credentials, she was free and rushing toward the staging area.

"Where is he?" she asked when she reached Matteo's side. The gleaming Viper was gorgeous, its red-and-white paint scheme shiny, the sponsor decals prominent against the surface. She expected Renzo to be standing proudly near the beast, but he was not.

Matteo shrugged. "Not sure, *signorina*. He was here a minute ago."

She turned in a circle, looking for the familiar racing leathers. But there were so many racing leathers, so many bright spots of color that caught her eye that she didn't think she would ever find him.

Her heart hammered in her breast and panic threaded

through her belly. Where was Renzo? Would he ever forgive her? Would she ever have the right to wrap her arms around him again?

And then she saw him, walking through the crowd toward the Viper, and her heart filled to bursting with love. She sprinted toward him, calling his name. He looked confused as he stopped. But then his eyes widened as he saw her, and his arms opened a split second before she crashed into them.

He smelled like leather and gasoline and she closed her eyes and hugged him tight. But then he pushed her back until he could see her, and she nearly burst into tears at the look on his face. He seemed…happy.

"Renzo, I—"

"Faith, I love you," he said, and her heart stopped. Literally stopped right there in the middle of the paddock with all the noise and craziness going on around them.

But it kicked hard again, lurching forward at double speed. She was dizzy. Dizzy and drunk with happiness and love.

"Did—did you just say…?"

He tugged her to him and captured her mouth, kissing her until her toes curled, kissing her until she could hear cheering and clapping all around them. She could see the flashes of cameras from behind her closed lids, but she didn't care. She didn't care what they reported about her anymore. So long as Renzo loved her, they could say any damn thing they wished and print any picture they wanted. She would never be ashamed again.

When he finally lifted his head, she clutched his arms for balance, her heart careening out of control with all she felt. But she still hadn't said what she'd come to say.

"Renzo, I want you to go out there and win. Do you understand? I want you to win."

He only smiled and slid his thumbs against her cheeks. "I don't care, *amore mia*. It's over, and I don't care. I'm not racing."

She blinked. "Is it—" She couldn't finish, so she glanced down to his leg, back up again.

He shook his head. "No. But you were right. I need to end it now. I need to retire and let someone else take the team to victory. I've had my time in the spotlight."

Her eyes filled with tears. "Please don't do this because of me. If you want to race, I want you to race. You've worked so hard." She tipped her head toward the men in cherry-red uniforms who were standing and watching them. "They've worked hard. If you want to take the Viper out, then don't stop because of me."

"I don't need the success anymore," he said. "I craved it because it was all I had, the only way to prove I was worthy...."

He didn't say anything for a long moment and she squeezed him tight. "*Cara*, everything I've done has been to prove that I was good enough to be my father's son. He may not acknowledge me, but by God he will know who I am and be sorry. I've let it rule me for far too long, and I no longer need it to validate my life." He smiled crookedly, and her heart broke for him. "I only need you."

"Oh Renzo, I understand."

"I know you do. We're alike, you and I. I know you've struggled with your feelings about your father. You've taught me that you just have to let it go at a certain point. It will always haunt me, but it doesn't have to rule me."

She squeezed him tight, her eyes flooding with tears. "Your father's a fool. A stupid, blind, ridiculous man who doesn't deserve you."

He laughed at her fierceness, but she meant it. "I know that, *cara*. Thanks to you."

There was an announcement of some kind, and then the teams began to move the motorcycles toward the starting grids. Matteo glanced over at them as he gave the order to move the Viper.

Renzo turned his head to watch them. She could see the spark in his eyes, the glint that said he was proud of the motorcycle and knew it would be amazing. And she wanted him to have this moment more than she wanted anything else. Because that's what you did when you loved someone.

She smiled at him through her tears. "Go, Renzo. It's okay. I swear it's okay. Just come back to me in forty-five minutes, you hear?"

He hesitated for a moment more. And then he bent and kissed her swiftly. "I will, Faith. I promise you I will."

EPILOGUE

THEY were married in the Duomo in Florence with one thousand of their friends and colleagues—as well as Renzo's mother and sister—packed inside the church. Outside in the square, thousands more gathered for the wedding of their favorite champion and his former PA. When Faith and Renzo emerged from the church, the crowd cheered in a loud, thundering rumble.

It sounded the same as when Renzo had been standing on top of that podium in Qatar, Faith thought. He'd won the race that day, and then he'd announced his retirement from MotoGP while a shocked crowd gasped and groaned.

But they'd forgiven him quickly, and the D'Angeli team was even now traveling the circuit and racking up wins on the Viper. The new production motorcycles had hit the dealerships, and business was booming.

Renzo tugged her into his arms and kissed her on the steps of the church, and then they were hurrying to the car that would take them back to the villa. Of all the places they could have honeymooned, that's where Faith wanted to be. Lola was there, and Fabrizio and Lucia. The vines were heavy with grapes that were ripening, the olive trees were bearing fruit, and the countryside was green during the day and golden in the evening. It was the most perfect place on earth, and she couldn't imagine another place in the world she would rather be.

They retreated to the bedroom where Renzo gave up patiently trying to divest her of her wedding gown and instead bunched the beautiful white taffeta around her hips as he held her against the wall and thrust into her urgently. It was the first time they'd made love without a barrier between them, and the sensation was exquisite.

They managed to undress, and then they fell into bed and lost themselves in each other's arms for the next few hours. Lucia brought dinner to the room, leaving it outside the door on a serving cart, and they sat on the private terrace overlooking the valley and ate. Faith was wearing a sheet and Renzo had slipped into a pair of briefs. It was as dressed as they would be for the next few days.

Renzo looked over from where he sat across from her in the evening light and smiled. "I love you, Signora D'Angeli," he said. "This is how I want to spend the rest of my life with you."

Faith laughed. "I love you too, Renzo. But you do have a very successful company to run."

He sighed. "And I need a new PA. I am not looking forward to finding one to replace you."

Faith bristled. "Replace me? I hardly think so, mister. You can't live without me, remember?"

"No," he said, smiling. "I can't. But you are my wife, not my PA. You won't always want to schedule my appointments and type my correspondence."

"I'm not particularly fond of typing correspondence," she admitted.

He grasped her hand and tugged her into his lap. The sheet slipped down her bosom, but she hardly cared, especially when his eyes flared with heat.

"You can be my PA as long as you want," he said. "And

when it's time to quit, you can interview the candidates if you like."

She put her arms around his neck and pressed herself closer to him. Oh, she was shameless when it came to wanting her gorgeous husband. "Since I'm the expert, yes. I would like that."

"There is only one condition," he said.

She reared back to look down at him. "What?"

"If I want you naked in my office, you have to comply."

Faith laughed. "What if I want *you* naked in your office? Does that work, too?"

She could feel him growing hard beneath her, and her body answered with a surge of heat between her thighs.

"What do you think?" he asked.

She wrapped her arms around his neck. "I think I'm going to enjoy working with you."

He kissed her hard, and then carried her into the bedroom. When they were entwined on the mattress, when he was deep inside her and she was begging him for more, he stopped and held still until her eyes opened.

"What is wrong, Renzo?"

He smiled. It was so full of tenderness and love that it made her heart ache. "Nothing is wrong," he said. "In fact, everything is right."

And it was. Faith knew that their lives together would be full and complete. They had each other, they had Lola—and several other stray cats that ended up making their way to the villa—and, nine months later, they had a screaming baby who refused to sleep through the night for at least a year.

It was chaos, but it was their chaos. And they wouldn't have it any other way.

* * * * *

MODERN™

INTERNATIONAL AFFAIRS, SEDUCTION & PASSION GUARANTEED

My wish list for next month's titles...

In stores from 20th July 2012:

☐ Contract with Consequences — Miranda Lee

☐ The Man She Shouldn't Crave — Lucy Ellis

☐ A Tainted Beauty — Sharon Kendrick

☐ The Dangerous Jacob Wilde — Sandra Marton

In stores from 3rd August 2012:

☐ The Sheikh's Last Gamble — Trish Morey

☐ The Girl He'd Overlooked — Cathy Williams

☐ One Night With The Enemy — Abby Green

☐ His Last Chance at Redemption — Michelle Conder

☐ The Hidden Heart of Rico Rossi — Kate Hardy

Available at WHSmith, Tesco, Asda, Eason, Amazon and Apple

Just can't wait?

Visit us Online

You can buy our books online a month before they hit the shops! **www.millsandboon.co.uk**

0712/0

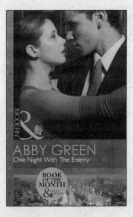

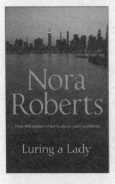